KNOCKED UP BY THE CEO

A SECRET BABY OFFICE ROMANCE

LILIAN MONROE

❀ Created with Vellum

1

HARPER

"COMING THROUGH!" I call out, balancing a tray of cookies in one hand and a jug of eggnog in the other. I can smell the boozy scent of rum coming off the eggnog and I know it'll be a big hit this year. My coworkers move out of the way as I crouch down towards the table and slide the tray off my hand onto the table in a smooth motion. The tablecloth is covered the cartoonish drawings of snowmen and snow flakes, with tinsel strewn under the trays of food. The whole office looks like the inside of a Christmas store. I place the jug of eggnog beside the cookies and stand up, putting my hands on my hips and turning around.

"That should be it," I breathe, pulling the hem of my sweater down. It's the ugliest and most amazing sweater I've ever seen, a wooly red monstrosity with flashing LED lights all over the front in the shape of a Christmas tree. Perfect for the office Christmas party.

"Well done, Harper! The place looks amazing," Rosie says as she walks up beside me. She's wearing her regular work clothes. In fact, no one except me is dressed up, but I don't mind. Rosie smiles and raises the plastic wine glass towards me. I grab a glass of my own from the dozens lined up on the table and lift it up it towards Rosie.

"I can finally start enjoying myself now," I grin back. We clink our glasses and I take my first sip of wine of the evening. "It's always so much work putting this party together."

"But it's always worth it," Rosie replies. "Think of all the gossip that comes out of it every year!"

She grins mischievously and takes another sip of wine, scanning the room over the rim of her glass. I laugh and nod. She's right, it's usually fodder for at least a couple months of water cooler chat. I've been in charge of the office Christmas party for the last three years, and they've gotten wilder as time has gone on. I'm sure this year will be the same.

"Nice sweatshirt!"

I try not to cringe as the screechy voice reaches my ears. The back of my neck prickles with that same uncomfortable feeling I get every time I hear his voice. I already know it's Greg from accounting. I turn around slowly and there he is, grinning at me with his toothy, slimy smile. I nod, trying not to stare at the stains on his tie or the greasy hair plastered to his forehead.

"Thanks," I respond curtly.

"You like Christmas, hey?"

"No, not really, I just do this so I can drink at the office."

He throws his head back and laughs before shuffling closer, his baggy pants and too-tight shirt sliding in beside me. I inch away as he gets closer. He smells like wet socks.

"Haven't seen you around the accounts department lately," he says to me. I try to avoid his stare and glance at Rosie. She's got her nose buried in her glass of wine.

"I got promoted a year ago, Greg. I don't work in accounts anymore."

"Yeah, yeah, of course, but you know, I thought you'd still come around and say hello to me—to the team. I thought we meant something to you!"

He smiles at me and I resist the urge to shudder. *I would rather come across as a cold-hearted snobby executive bitch than to willingly spend time with you, after all the torture you put me through!* Greg glances at Rosie and his smile disappears immediately. He almost snarls at her and I grab her arm and point over to the other side of the room.

"Oh, look, it looks like those decorations need to be adjusted. Excuse me."

"I'll help!" Rosie says. The two of us speed away towards the huge tree I rented for the party.

"Is he still following you around? I thought you'd made a complaint."

I sigh. "I did, he got a warning from HR and avoided me for a while but it looks like he's plucked up the courage to talk to me again. Might be the booze."

"Isn't there anything you can do? He *followed* you to your *house*! Multiple times!"

"Don't remind me," I say, glancing at her sideways. I push the thought away, not wanting to go back to those months last year when I was constantly looking over my shoulder. I didn't even know it was Greg until weeks after the whole thing started. I spent weeks and weeks with that same prickly feeling at the back of my neck, feeling like I was being followed and thinking I was going insane.

The promotion to Commercial Director came with a healthy pay raise and the condition that my complaint about Greg would be satisfied when he got a warning. I never

3

understood why the Human Resources department didn't take me more seriously, but at the end of the day not many women make it to the Director-level at a top advertising firm at my age. I weighed my options and for the most part, it was worth it. I hardly have to see him anyways.

Rosie and I get to the Christmas tree and look at all 16 feet of it. The top of it grazes the ceiling.

"So what do you want us to adjust? I think Greg is still looking over here," Rosie asks, looking at the massive tree. It was almost too big to fit in the door. I had to beg and plead to get approval for it, saying that it wasn't a Christmas party without a tree. It's impeccably decorated and I already know that nothing needs to be adjusted.

"Uh, let's just lift this string of lights a bit. We can just move them around till he looks away."

I point to the other side of the tree and Rosie nods. I turn to the lights and am about to grab them when she makes a noise between a gasp and a yelp and I look at her. Her eyes are staring behind me before she flicks them to my face. She lifts her eyebrows up and gives me a knowing nod.

It must be *him*. Immediately my heart starts beating faster and I hear the roar of every heartbeat pounding in my ears.

It's our elusive, mysterious, unbelievably sexy CEO. Zachary Lockwood. I feel my cheeks burning as Rosie glances back at him. I turn my head slowly and see him near the entrance of the office, shaking hands with one of the employees. His suit is navy with little white pinstripes. His chocolate brown hair is slicked back perfectly, with a crisp part down the side. He's tall and athletic, with a chiseled jaw and unbelievably deep brown eyes. Not that I've noticed, or anything.

I glance away quickly, trying to ignore the thumping of

my heart. I've been admiring him from a distance ever since he took over and brought our firm back from the brink of bankruptcy. Rosie knows it, and constantly teases me whenever he makes an appearance at the office. Thankfully that doesn't happen very often.

"He doesn't have a hot blonde model with him this time, maybe this is your chance!" Rosie whispers loudly with a grin.

"Shut up," I respond. "I'm sure he's got a gaggle of girls waiting in the wings."

Rosie nods and my heart sinks a little. I know it's probably true. He's one of the richest and sexiest men in New York, and definitely way, way out of my league. Plus, he's my boss! Even if I had a chance with him, it would definitely be inappropriate to pursue it.

Suddenly I wish I wasn't wearing a ridiculous light-up Christmas tree on my chest. I could be wearing anything else and it would be more flattering. Literally *anything*. A paper bag would look better than this thing.

It doesn't matter, I tell myself. He's my boss. Even if he is attractive, we work together and fantasising about him is inappropriate. I shake my head and try to ignore the nervous excitement at the pit of my stomach. I take another sip of wine and nod to Rosie and the string of lights. She grins but says nothing, and instead turns to the tree and follows my lead.

2

ZACH

I'VE BEEN TRYING NOT to stare at her ever since I walked in. Harper Anderson *is* my employee, after all. I can't help it that there's something about her that intrigues me. Maybe it's the way she doesn't seem to care who I am? Usually employees, especially women, are nervous and flustered when they see me. She's all business, all the time. Nothing seems to phase her.

I glance over at her as she talks to another woman beside the massive fake Christmas tree that dominates the room. She marched into my office six weeks ago and insisted on ordering that huge tree, standing in front of me with a graph she'd prepared that showed Christmas cheer increasing exponentially with every extra foot of tree that we ordered. Her face had been so serious, and she'd presented her carefully prepared graphs and figures as if it was the quarterly review.

I had no choice, I had to say yes. Harper had me totally off-balance and I hadn't even been able to laugh at the ridiculousness and thoroughness of her proposal. But as soon as I said yes I'd seen a twinkle in her eye and I knew there was something different about her. It's not often that people surprise me like that.

She's good at what she does, and that's what matters. It doesn't matter that my cock starts to twitch whenever I think about her, or that I can't seem to get her out of my head for days every time I visit the office.

"... the Jackson file will be ready for your signature by Monday morning, and.. Zach? Are you listening?"

I'm pulled from my thoughts and turn towards my Editor in Chief and best friend. I put a hand on his shoulder and look him in the eye.

"Mitch. It's the Christmas party. No more work talk."

"Alright, alright," he says, throwing his hands up. "You want a drink?" he asks, motioning towards the snack table.

I nod as I glance at the full spread of food and drink on the table. Harper's done a good job this year, once again. There's every imaginable snack and appetiser and drink that anyone could ever want. The woman knows how to throw a party.

Mitch starts walking towards the drinks. "You got any plans this weekend?"

"I was thinking of checking out that new club downtown tomorrow night, you in? There's a potential client there with a VIP booth."

Mitch grins. "VIP booth means girls girls girls. I'm in."

I nod. He's right, there will be women. There always are, at these things. It's part of the job, really. Our brand is what sells advertisements—luxury, excess, riches, women, everything that's good in the world. Everything that's good in my life. I see people my age settling down and having kids and all I can think is *why?!* Why would you want that? Why would you want to be tied to one person for the rest of your life?

"What happened with that model you were seeing? I thought you'd be here with her," Mitch asks as we get to the table. There are dozens of tiny wine glasses lined up in front of us.

"Didn't work out," I reply. It never does. I never let it, women just want to use me for my money and status, so I use them right back.

"Tomorrow is a new night," Mitch says as he hands me a glass of wine.

"Tonight is a new night," I correct with a grin. He chuckles and nods before taking a sip. I drink with him but something is off. I don't quite believe myself when I say these things tonight. Why would I care about models and actresses and all these beautiful women that only want me for what I can buy for them, or who I can introduce them to? Maybe the people settling down have found something I haven't.

Probably not. I grab a glass of wine off the table.

"Merry Christmas," I say to Mitch.

"Merry Christmas, buddy. To every night being a new night, and every girl being a new girl!"

I force a chuckle and touch my glass to his. I steal another glance over towards Harper. She's laughing at something. I can see her cheeks flushing from over here. I can't quite make out her freckles, but if I get a little bit closer I'm sure I could see them scattered over her cheeks and nose. She's completely dwarfed standing next to that ridiculous tree. She's wearing an atrocious red sweater with lights on it, pointing to the decorations with the woman next to her. I have no idea how, but somehow she makes it look sexy.

She's smiling at her friend and the two of them laugh

about something. Her sweater is flashing and I almost let myself grin as I look at her. Just as Mitch and I start walking away from the drinks she turns her head and our eyes meet from across the room.

It only lasts a second before she looks away but something stirs inside me. Those green eyes of hers are like beams of light that pierce right through me. I could see that twinkle in her eye from all the way over here and I can't help but wonder what she's laughing about.

I need to get closer to her tonight, to have an actual conversation with her. I'm not going to settle for the same business talk and cold mask that she puts on. I want to know the real Harper Anderson.

HARPER

HE WAS LOOKING RIGHT at me. My heart is practically jumping out of my chest. *Get it together!* I've only had half a glass of wine and I'm already dizzy from one look. Who cares how good looking he is?! He's a player! And he's *my boss.*

I glance at Rosie and nod towards the lights. She grabs the strand of wire and we lift it away from the tree together. We move it up a fraction of an inch and then place it back down on the fake green branches. It looks exactly the same.

"There," I say with exaggerated satisfaction, dusting my hands off in front of me. Rosie laughs. I glance at her and grin before turning back to the tree. At least it got me away from Greg.

"It looks perfect, Harps," Rosie says. I can tell she means it.

"It better look perfect, it's costing old Mister Zachary Moneybags a small fortune," I laugh. "I still can't believe he approved the expense."

My eyes drift upwards and I notice that one of the bow-shaped ribbons is caught in a branch and twisted awkwardly. I reach up towards it, trying to wiggle it loose. It's almost out of reach. I can just touch it with the tips of my fingers as I stand on the tip of my toes.

I take a small step forward and try to reach the bow again. The soft velvet of the bow tickles my fingertips and I stretch my body a tiny bit more until I can grasp it between two fingers.

"Come on," I breathe, grabbing it and pulling it down to straighten it out. I have the bow in my fingers and pull gently, but something is wrong. It's not budging as easily as I thought it would. I try yanking it a little bit harder to bring the bow out from the branches. I'm on the tips of my toes, taking a thousand tiny steps forward and back to keep my balance. I grab the bow once more between my fingers and pull just a tiny, tiny bit harder.

The bow wrenches loose and I finally get a grip on it, and then everything happens at once. I try to fix the ribbon but something is wrong. I'm still on the tips of my toes and I feel like the ground is shifting under my feet and I can't regain my balance. My feet shuffle forward and back again a million times. My stomach drops and time slows down.

No, no, no, no, no!

"Harper!" I hear Rosie's voice as if it's coming at me from underwater. I hear her scream as I feel myself falling backwards, still grabbing on to that pesky velvet ribbon between my fingers. My heart leaps into my throat as I feel the ground falling away from me, sending me flying backwards. I'm spinning, falling through the air in slow motion. Finally I let go of that stupid bow and my arms fly up towards my head to protect my fall.

I hit the ground with a thud and the air gets knocked out of my lungs. My eyes are closed and the pain of the landing jolts through my body.

I land a second before the tree does. Before I know what's happening, there's a deafening series of smashes and crunches and shattering of ornaments all around me as the plastic branches collapse on top of me. All sixteen feet of the massive, expensive, unnecessary Christmas tree that I insisted on ordering falls down on top of me with an earth-shattering crash.

It takes a second for me to realise what's happened. Miraculously I haven't been impaled, but all I can see are green branches and shattered ornaments all around me. I'm pinned under the tree. I can't move. When the ringing in my ears quiets down I hear shouting and screaming from my coworkers and I close my eyes, sighing deeply.

Oh. My. God.

The reality of what's just happened slowly dawns on me as I lay there, trapped by my own decorations. There's a plastic pine branch rubbing against my cheek and a hard ornament digging into my leg. I try to move my leg but all I can do is wiggle my foot back and forth. I'm well and truly stuck. I close my eyes and try to catch my breath.

I've just tipped over the sixteen-foot tree on top of myself at the annual Christmas party, in front of every single employee and all my bosses. In front of *him*—in front of Zach *freaking Lockwood!* The embarrassment is almost too much to bear. I lay my head down on the hard floor and close my eyes, trying to ignore the thumping of my heart and the burning in my cheeks.

Rosie's voice calls out. "Harper! Are you okay?!" She

sounds panicked. I try to answer but nothing comes out, so I clear my throat and try again.

"Yep, yeah. Yeah, I'm fine." I answer, trying to keep my voice steady. *I'm fine. I'm great, even. Fantastic. Never better.*

4

ZACH

I LIFT my head just as the tree is tipping past the point of no return and I watch in stunned horror as Harper falls backwards, pulling the tree down on top of her. It crashes down within seconds, sending ornaments and lights flying across the room. The top of it lands on top of the food table, knocking it over and sending snacks and drinks crashing to the ground.

Within seconds I'm beside the tree, trying to lift it off her.

"You," I point to a man next to me. "Grab that branch. You," I point to a woman near the tip of the tree. "Grab the trunk. On three. One, two, three!"

A dozen of us grunt as we lift the tree back up. This thing weighs about a thousand pounds. It takes half a dozen of us to get it upright again as broken ornaments and tinsel rain down on top of us.

Once it's lifted back upright I glance down and see Harper on the floor. She looks stunned, laying on her back as she watches us get the tree upright again. An ornament bounces off the tree and rolls over beside her. She picks it up and looks at it blankly. I walk over and crouch down, balancing on my heels as I squat next to her. Her eyes are hazy and her cheeks are flushed. Her auburn hair is a bird's nest and she has tinsel and broken Christmas ornaments littered all over her. The lights on her sweater are still blinking.

"You alright, Harper?"

She nods.

"Yeah, I'm fine," she responds. As soon as I hear her speak I feel a desperate urge to laugh but I keep my best poker face on. She tries to sit up and groans, pausing to balance herself on her elbows. I reach down and grab her arm, helping her to her feet. The second my hand touches her arm I feel something like a spark go off inside me. My cock twitches but I ignore it, brushing broken glass off Harper's shoulder.

I watch as she glances around the room at the circle of coworkers that has formed around us. Harper stands up a bit straighter and raises her arms slowly, as if to acknowledge the crowd. An embarrassed grin creeps over her face and I can't help but notice how it makes her eyes sparkle that little bit brighter.

A cheer and a laugh starts rippling through the crowd and suddenly everyone is clapping. Harper takes a small bow and I see her stumble a little. I grab her arm a bit tighter and help her up. I can feel her shaking and I keep my hand on her arm to hold her steady. I've never been this close to her.

I glance around the office. It's absolute carnage. There's decorations, food, spilled juice and wine and eggnog all over the place. The food table is knocked over onto its side and all the refreshments are soaking into the thin office carpet. Harper is still shaking and people are starting to come closer to us. I wave to my assistant who rushes over.

"Becca, here's my credit card." I turn to the crowd. Almost every single person employed by the company is here, watching Harper and I, still laughing and cheering. I hold up my hand and the place quiets down. "Alright everyone, the venue has changed. Open bar at the regular spot downstairs, compliments of the company. Harper and I will be down in a few minutes. Happy Holidays!"

There's a cheer and clapping.

"Nice one, Harper! Best Christmas party yet!" Another wave of laughter ripples through the crowd and people start filing out. One woman, I forget her name, steps forward. She goes to Harper.

"You okay, Harps?" Harper smiles again. I'm still holding her upright and I can feel how weak she is.

"I'm fine, just a bit shaken up. Thanks, Zach," she says as she pulls her arm away. I reluctantly let go and take a step back. It feels like a chasm between us. Harper turns to the woman. "I'll be down in a bit, Rosie. You go enjoy yourself." *Rosie, that's it. One of our junior editors.*

"I'll stay here and help you!"

"No, no, it's fine, really. I'll be down in a few minutes." I watch as Rosie nods slowly and then glances at me before nodding and turning around.

"Come on, sit down," I say gently, guiding Harper to a chair nearby. She sits down heavily and puts her forehead in her hand, slouching down. Her sweater crumples slightly at the front. The lights are still twinkling in the shape of a tree all over her torso. It truly is one of the ugliest sweaters I've ever seen.

"I can't believe I just did that," she says. I can sense the embarrassment radiating off her. A smile starts creeping across my face.

"I can't believe you did that either," I respond. She glances at me through her fingers and I can't help it. I start laughing, a deep, booming belly laugh. It starts in my stomach and consumes my entire body until my shoulders are shaking and my cheeks hurt. I haven't laughed like this in a long time. After a few moments I watch as Harper's shoulders relax and she starts smiling and finally laughing with me.

She sighs deeply and then glances beside her. There's an abandoned half glass of wine. I watch as she takes it between her delicate fingers and shrugs as if to say, 'why not!' before pouring the whole thing into her mouth. This is definitely a side of her I haven't seen before. I glance over and see the bottles of wine near the upturned table. I walk over and grab one of them and another glass then head back to Harper and pull up a chair.

"Merry Christmas," I say as I fill both our glasses. "This might be our most expensive Christmas party yet. Hope this was in your budget," I tease, sweeping my arm towards the wreckage.

"Zach... I..."

I hold up my hand. "Don't. It's okay. At least people will be talking about you this year and not me. Last year I think I heard every rumour in the book about my love life." I pause and glance at Harper. "Or lack thereof."

She grins and sighs again, shaking her head. "Well don't worry, I've got the gossip covered this year." She glances at the tree, which is now upright and more than a little crooked. There's a few snapped branches littered on the floor. "I just had to get the biggest tree I could find, didn't I."

"Sixteen feet tall!" I breathe in mock amazement. I glance over and see that smile spread across her face. She chuckles silently and then takes a sip of wine, looking at me over the edge of her glass.

Something stirs inside me as her eyes flick to mine. I never noticed the light in them before. I clear my throat and glance back at my wine, filling up both our glasses up and clinking mine against hers.

Somehow the air seems thicker than before. I can sense every move that Harper is making and the way her eyes are burning into me is making my cock stir in my pants. I shift in my seat and clear my throat again before taking another sip of wine.

5

HARPER

I'VE NEVER SPENT this much time with him. Usually Zach is in and out of the office and it's all business with him. He spends his time doing who knows what with clients—networking, I guess—and leaves the actual operation of the business to us. I watch the way he's reclining on the chair, bringing the plastic wine glass to his red lips. I wonder what his lips would taste like?

I glance away and try to shake the thought from my head. This wine must be getting to me, or maybe it was the adrenaline of the fall. This is my boss! Not only that, this is the CEO of the whole company!! It's probably inappropriate for me to be here alone drinking with him. It's *definitely* inappropriate for me to be thinking about kissing him.

Still, there's something exciting about it. My eyes dart back to him and a thrill rushes down my spine when I see he's looking at me. Why did I have to wear this stupid sweatshirt?? As if reading my mind, Zach asks me:

"Where'd you get your sweater? It's very... unique." He

grins and raises an eyebrow. I look down and gently touch the twinkling LEDs on my torso.

"I got it at a Goodwill. It was three dollars."

"Wow, what a bargain," he responds. I nod, grinning proudly.

"Didn't even have to buy any batteries for it!" This time he laughs, a deep belly laugh that makes his shoulders shake. I notice the way his smile lights his whole face up and his eyes close as he tilts his head back to laugh. He has perfect teeth. His laugh sends a wave of heat through me and I can't help but giggle along. It feels good to be here with him, like this.

Zach's laugh dies down and he grins at me. "I never knew this side of you." He's staring at me intently, as if he's looking through me or into me, trying to figure me out. "You always seem so serious and professional." I resist the urge to squirm. Instead, I turn to the fallen tree.

"What, *this* side of me?" I ask, sweeping my arm towards the mess of snacks and drinks and upturned furniture. "Now that you see it, are you impressed? Personally I think clumsiness is irresistible."

I bring the the wine glass up to my lips and raise my eyebrow, watching his face as I take a sip. My heart is thumping as he watches me, a subtle smile playing on his lips.

"Irresistible is one word for it," he responds in a low voice. I can feel the rumble of his voice in my bones, like it traveled straight through me. It doesn't sound like he's joking. A warmth starts spreading in my centre and I desperately want to reach over and touch him, grab him, feel his hand or his arm or anything. I want to feel his arms around me and breathe in his smell.

Instead I stay rooted to my chair. We watch each other

without moving. The tension is palpable, and I can hardly breathe for fear of breaking the spell that's cast over us. Zach looks towards the fallen table and slowly gets up. He rolls up the sleeves of his shirt to reveal his sinewy forearms. I lick my lips. I watch as he walks towards the mess, his crisp white shirt tucked into his pinstriped trousers. His back looks wide and strong, and I can see the outline of his shoulders through the thin white fabric. I watch him crouch down and pick up the table, setting it back upright.

I get up and follow him over. I start a few feet away from him, picking up boxes and cookies and cakes that have fallen on the floor. We work in silence for a few minutes. I stand up after picking up the millionth item off the floor, wiping a bead of sweat from my forehead. I grab my heavy sweater and pull it off over my head, letting out a sigh.

"It's hot in here!" I exclaim, and then I see Zach's eyes on me. His eyes are roaming over me and suddenly I feel like I'm wearing nothing at all. I pull down the hem of my thin camisole. I wasn't intending on taking off my sweater. I blush and turn back to the mess on the floor to hide my embarrassment. I bend over to pick up a stack of plastic plates and when I stand up he's right beside me, his arm brushing against mine. He turns towards me so that his chest is inches from mine.

I place the plates down gently on the table and try to slow down the thumping in my chest. Zach is so close to me I can feel the heat radiating off his skin. He smells sweet and spicy at the same time and I breathe deeply, trying to calm myself down. As soon as his scent hits my nostrils it has the opposite effect. My body goes into overdrive and all I can think of is putting my hands on his body.

We're inches apart. Slowly, I drag my eyes up his chest to

his jaw, watch his lips as he opens them gently and finally let my eyes drift up to his. They look so dark, like bottomless pools of brown staring back at me.

My heart is going wild. I can feel it beating against my ribcage as we stand there, transfixed. I can't tear my eyes away from his. I don't want to.

Ever so slowly, Zach brings his hand up and gently brushes the edge of my hip with his fingertips. I shiver, closing my eyes gently and relishing his touch. He's barely touching me but it feels more intense than I could imagine. It's like his fingers have a direct line to my centre, sending wave after wave of heat towards my core.

His fingers drift from my hip towards my navel, ever so gently brushing the fabric of my camisole. The blood is rushing between my legs and desire floods my veins with every heartbeat banging against my ribcage. I open my eyes and glance back at him. His eyes are half-closed. I can see him looking at me and the intensity of his gaze sends another wave of heat through me. I know my eyes have the same look of pure desire as his. I raise my hand and hesitate, then place it gently on his chest. He's warm, and hard, his smooth muscles rippling under his shirt. I can feel his heart beating as well and it gives me a surge of confidence. My other hand flies up to his chest and I run it up towards his neck.

The second my fingers touch the bare skin of his neck it's like something explodes between us. My skin touches his and it sizzles, sending sparks through my entire body. He grips my waist and pulls me into him.

This is so wrong. This is my boss! Zach Lockwood! I shouldn't be doing this.

But then his lips crush against mine and all thought disappears from my head. He tastes sweet, his lips soft against mine as they part and kiss me. His hand grips my neck, tangling into the hair at the nape of my neck and pulling my head in towards his. My hands are gripping his shoulders, his neck, grabbing his shirt and pulling him into me.

He's pressing me into the table and I lean back, loving the way his body feels strong and muscular as he crushes it into me. His lips press against my neck, trailing kisses down my collarbone as his hands grab the small of my back and pull me into him. I'm panting, trying to keep my feet on the ground as my body goes into overdrive. The pleasure and desire is exploding through my entire body and I can feel my wetness pooling between my legs.

I want him. I don't care that he's my boss, or the CEO, or that we're at the office. I want him more than I've ever wanted anyone before.

6

ZACH

THE MINUTE she took that sweater off I knew I had to kiss her. My cock started throbbing as soon as I laid eyes on her, and now she's here in my arms and it feels better than I could have imagined. She's pulling me into her and kissing me like I'm the last man on Earth. Right now, here with Harper, I might as well be. The office is a mess and it's going to cost me a fortune to fix everything up and pay for the office party at the pub but I don't care. I'd pay ten times whatever it costs to be exactly where I am now.

I grab the tops of her thighs and lift her onto the table, sending a box of cookies flying back down to the ground as I brush it out of the way. She wraps her arms around my neck and pulls me down on top of her. We're both panting, clawing at each other, grabbing and pulling at whatever body part our hands can find.

"Wait," Harper says, pulling away. "Anyone could walk in."

"I don't care," I breathe. "Let them watch."

I kiss her again. I can't think of anything except the way

she tastes, the way she feels, and the way my cock is straining against my pants and throbbing like it's about to explode. I feel her hands on my chest and she gently pushes me away again. I nod.

"You're right. Come on."

I help her off the table and she slips her hand into mine. We head towards my office. It's just on the other end of the room, in the back corner. As soon as we're in the door she slams the door closed and jumps into my arms. She wraps her legs around my waist and I wrap my arms around her, our lips already crushing together the minute the door slammed shut. I walk over to the couch that faces the big bay windows and set her down gently onto it. I love this view— New York's twinkling city lights—but right now I can't look at anything except the beautiful woman laying down in front of me.

Her cheeks are flushed and she has that twinkle in her eyes. They look like emeralds, bright even in the dim light of the office. I can see her freckles now, scattered over her face. I brush my thumb over her cheek.

"You are incredibly sexy," I breathe as my lips dip down to kiss her collarbone. Her hands reach up and tangle into my hair.

"I bet you say that to all the girls," she teases. I lift my head and grin.

"Yeah, I do," I admit. "But this time I actually mean it." She laughs and I get to see that smile spreading across her face. Her eyes are so bright, every look is sending an electric thrill straight down to my cock. I lean down and kiss her neck again. I can't get enough of her soft white skin. She grinds her hips upwards and I groan, loving the way her body feels underneath me.

Suddenly Harper tenses and looks over my shoulder. "What was that?!"

I glance back and look towards the door. "What?"

"I heard something. I think someone's here." Her voice sounds strained and her heart is beating fast. I can feel it as I lay there on top of her. She's tensed up completely and the whites of her eyes are visible all around her irises. I frown, slowly lifting myself off the couch. I can't help but feel Harper's nervousness.

Was that a shadow I just saw through the blinds? They're mostly shut but if someone was close enough they could see in. At least, they could see enough to know what we were just doing. My heart jumps in my chest and I feel the blood start to pound through my veins. I get up and take a few steps towards the door, pausing to listen. Silence.

I reach forward, grabbing the door handle in my right hand. With one last breath, I clench my other fist and rip the door open.

Nothing. It's empty.

"Hello?" I call out. "Who's there?"

I wait for one, two, three seconds, taking a step out into the open room and listening for any sound.

It's completely quiet. I take a few more steps and look around. The room is exactly as we left it: a complete mess. I squint and try to look for movement, any movement, around the room. There's nothing. No sound, no movement, nothing.

Sighing, I turn back around. I walk back into my office and close the door. I hold my arms out by my sides and shrug. Harper is looking at me, wide-eyed. She's sitting up on the couch now, her arms by her side. Her hair is messy and her cheeks are flushed.

"Nothing," I say simply. I turn to the blinds and close

them shut completely, just in case. Then I turn back to Harper and we look at each other for a few seconds. She's never looked this good.

She's the first to start smiling. It starts as the corners of her mouth start twitching upwards, and then her eyes brighten. Suddenly she's laughing, looking at me and holding her chest as the laughter barrels out of her. I can't help it, I start laughing too.

My shoulders shake and I lean back, letting the stress of the past few moments roll off me. I collapse onto the sofa next to her and lean back, laughing until it subsides and we both sigh. Harper turns to me and looks me in the eye, her eyes shining.

"Sorry," she says. "Guess I'm a bit nervous. Sex in the office and all."

Before I can respond, she's got her hand on my chest and is crushing her lips against mine. She swings her leg over me and straddles my thighs. I let my hands drift from her hips down to her ass, loving the way it curves under my touch. She starts grinding herself into me and I groan. My cock is rock hard. I can't wait any longer. I need her. I need to make her mine.

7

HARPER

ONCE THE STRESS DISSIPATED, I had to lean over and kiss him. And now I feel completely out of control in the best possible way.

I can't help myself, his lips taste so good. The way he's grabbing my hips and ass, pulling me down on top of him is driving me crazy. I can feel his hard cock in his pants, pressing against my leg as I move up and down on top of him.

I push myself off and stand up, hastily unfastening my pants. I slide them down my legs and stand up. I can't wait any longer, this is happening. I hear Zach sigh and I look at him. He's staring at me with fire in his eyes. He's unbuckling his belt and sliding his pants down. We're both rushing, clawing at our clothes and ripping them off.

I can't wait for him to take them off. As soon as they're bunched near his feat I climb back on top of him and grab his cock in my hand. It's thick and hard, and even the touch of it makes my body shiver with pleasure. I put one hand on his shoulder and stare at him. His dark brown eyes are boring into me and I don't look away for a moment as I take his cock and slowly start moving it back and forth along my slit.

Every time it comes near my opening or my bud it sends a thrill through my entire body. I can feel my body opening up, getting sopping wet and ready for him. I don't remember the last time I wanted a man this badly. His hands are on me, his fingers sinking into my ass as I move slowly back and forth.

The way he's groaning is driving me wild. I don't know if it's the wine or the nervousness or the sheer thrill of being at the office like this with the man I've been fantasising about for weeks, but I can feel my orgasm mounting before he's even done anything to me. Just the way his hands grip me, the way his groans pierce through me, the way his body feels smooth and hard is enough to take me to the edge.

I can't take it anymore. I feel drunk, but not off alcohol. I close my eyes and shift my hips, still grabbing his cock as I position it underneath me.

Sinking down onto his cock is the most erotic thing I've ever felt. Inch by inch, he slides inside me like his cock was made to be there. I can feel my body stretching and gripping and contracting as he enters me. I moan, sitting down completely on top of him. I exhale as I sit back. Finally I open my eyes and look down at him.

His mouth is open and he's exhaling, his eyes shining in the dim light as he watches me. He lets out a low groan and I shiver, taking a second to let my body adjust to his size. His fingers sink into my ass a little bit more and I can feel his cock throbbing inside me.

Every sensation is heightened. Every touch sends shivers through my whole body. Every heartbeat makes the pleasure course through my veins a little bit more. I take a deep breath and start grinding my hips, slowly at first and then faster and faster.

Suddenly it's a frenzy. I'm grinding and riding and bucking and he's thrusting into me, grabbing my ass and my neck and my hair as he pushes himself deeper into me. Our bodies are slapping together and our moans fill the room.

I feel almost dizzy. It's intoxicating—the feeling of him inside me. Every time my hips sink down and his cock pushes into me it's like a bolt of lightening through my core. The pressure inside me is building and building and building until I can feel my orgasm inside me like a ball of heat that's ready to explode.

The instant he slips his hand between us and finds my clit it's all over. I'm flying through space, eyes closed, body bucking and convulsing in pleasure as he grinds into me more. I'm screaming his name but it's like the sound of my own voice reaches my ears a second too late. My walls are contracting around his cock as our bodies crush together. I can feel him groaning and moaning, grabbing my hips and pushing himself into me a little bit deeper.

His cock gets harder and hotter and all of a sudden I feel him explode. We come together, our bodies completely in sync as we moan and grab onto each other tightly.

My heart is pounding and I collapse on top of Zach. His breath is ragged, and his arms fall down by his sides. My walls are still twitching, gripping and releasing his cock inside me with every beat of my heart. His cock is pulsing and all we can do is sit there until our bodies recover.

Slowly, I climb off him and sink onto the sofa beside him. His arm is around my shoulder, his fingers lazily trailing over and back across my skin. I lay my head against him and I feel him lay a soft kiss against my hair.

"You smell nice," he breathes. I smile.

"So do you," I respond. I take a deep breath and lay into him a little bit more. I smile to myself as we enjoy a quiet moment.

My thoughts are buzzing even though my body is relaxed. This is completely out of character for me. I just had sex at the office *with my boss*!! Not only that, but were in such a rush that we didn't use any protection. I sigh, I know the chances of me getting pregnant are pretty much zero. I discovered that right before my last relationship crashed and burned, after months of appointments and treatments and tests. It was heartbreaking, but I've accepted it now. I'll never have kids of my own.

I try to quiet my mind down and focus on Zach's chest and the way his fingers are trailing back and forth on my shoulder. Right now I'm not going to let my thoughts run away with me. All I can do is close my eyes and enjoy Zach's body wrapped around mine. His breath is slow and his heartbeat is steady and it feels like the most comfortable place I've ever been. I sigh gently and settle into him.

A couple hours ago I never would have imagined that I'd be half-naked in Zach Lockwood's office enjoying the afterglow of an intense orgasm. Maybe pulling the tree down wasn't such a disaster after all.

8

ZACH

"WE SHOULD PROBABLY GO to the Christmas party. They'll be wondering where we are," Harper says as her head lies against my shoulder. She makes no move to leave.

"Probably, yeah," I respond, staying completely still. It's too comfortable here. It feels too good to have my arm wrapped around her and to feel the little shocks course through my veins as my body recovers from my orgasm. Harper shivers and sighs against me, then finally lifts herself off.

I watch her bend over and pick up her discarded pants, loving the way her ass curves into her shapely legs. She's got to be one of the sexiest women I've ever seen. My head still feels light, like I've had one too many drinks. I know it's not the alcohol though, I feel such a rush through my body the second she sank down on top of my cock.

Sighing, I bend down and pull my pants back up my legs. Harper shoots me a glance and grins.

"That was fun," she says. I smile.

"Yeah." I pause, unsure how to ask her what I'm thinking

of. "Harper, we never used... I didn't have a condom. I'm clean! It's just..."

Harper's face tightens and she nods. Her eyes cloud over as if she's thinking of something painful and then she stands tall and shakes her head. "I won't get pregnant, if that's what you're worried about. I... I don't usually do that."

She waves her hand towards the couch. She looks almost worried, even though it's done. I know people say that all the time but I believe her. The way we had sex was far too real, far too instinctual to be some regular one-night stand for her. I hope so, anyway. Was that a one night stand?

"Don't usually do what, sleep with your boss? Pull down a gigantic Christmas tree? Fuck like your life depended on it?"

She laughs. "Yeah, something like that. It's been a long time since..." her voice trails off and she looks down at the ground. She's wringing her hands, suddenly lost in thought. I take a step towards her and put my arms around her waist, lifting my hand to tilt her chin up towards me. Her lips are soft when they touch mine, and they open slightly so I can taste her mouth. She shivers in my arms and we stay like that for a minute before pulling apart.

"We should go," I whisper. She nods and pulls away from me, smoothing her shirt down. Our bodies separate and it feels wrong. I want to put my arm around her, grab her hand, inhale her scent, but I can't. It's over now, I can feel it. Harper's body goes a little bit rigid and she puts on the familiar professional air that I've seen from her at work.

We head out of the office and Harper heads towards the table. There's still spilled food and drink all around. She grabs her red sweater and pulls it on overhead. She fiddles with the hem and the lights turn back on, flashing on her torso in the shape of a Christmas tree. I laugh.

"That thing is ridiculous."

"I know," she says proudly, spinning and posing for me as she laughs.

Suddenly she stops and looks down at her feet. She frowns and I look down to see what she's staring at. Harper bends over slowly and gathers a pile of plastic plates on the ground. She's crouching down, holding them in her hands and staring at them intently. She looks back at me, her eyes betraying a hint of panic.

"I picked these up before. I put them on the table in a stack right before we..." She looks between me and the plates, standing up slowly. "I thought I heard someone, or something fall over."

She holds up the plates and then looks back up at me and I can see the worry in her face. I close the distance between us and take the plates gently out of her hands, putting them on the table.

"They could have fallen when we were out here," I say. "We weren't exactly careful when I had you on the table. Maybe they were on the edge and fell off the table on their own."

She doesn't look convinced so I continue.

"No one was here, Harper. Don't worry." She flicks those emerald eyes back up at me and smiles weakly, nodding her chin down once.

"You're right," she says with a sigh. "I've just worked hard to get to where I am I'd hate something like this to ruin it."

She waves her hand dismissively when she says *something like this*. For some reason it stings, the way she waved it away. As if sleeping with me was a mistake and she's already trying to forget about it.

I push the feeling down. What do I care? Of course this

isn't anything serious! I've never wanted anything serious with anyone, ever. If she's thinking of it as a casual fling then that's the best thing for the both of us. The worst thing either of us could do is get attached.

"Don't worry Harper, this won't ruin anything. I should tell you, I'm not looking for anything.. serious." I tell her. She holds up her hand to stop me.

"Zach, please. We're adults. We wanted to sleep together and we did. I think that we can agree that it stops there, and we can go back to being professionals."

I nod, but I can't help but feel disappointed at how eagerly she agreed. Why did that sting? It's what I want!

Harper sighs and smiles at me. "That's settled then. Let's go downstairs," she says. "We can see if the bar has any Christmas trees that need to be tipped over."

She grins and nods her head towards the elevators. Her eyes glimmer and I resist the urge to lean over and kiss her. I nod back and the two of us head down to join the rest of the staff.

9

HARPER

THE WHOLE PUB cheers when we walk in. My cheeks turn bright red immediately, and I curse my genetics for making me so quick to blush. I lift my arms up and the cheers get louder, and suddenly I'm surrounded by my coworkers who are clapping me on the back and congratulating me.

"Best office party entertainment in years, Harper! Well done!"

"I wish was filming it!"

"You couldn't have done it better if you'd planned it!"

I roll my eyes and laugh, looking beside me to glance at Zach only to realise he's left my side. I scan the crowd and frown for a moment before seeing him at the bar. He has his back turned to me and is talking to the pretty girl behind the bar. I feel a sting in my chest before Rosie materialises beside me and grabs me by the elbow, pulling me away from the crowd.

"What took you so long?" She asks, staring at me intently. "You guys were up there for ages."

There I go blushing again. I shrug.

"Just talked and then cleaned up a bit. The office is a mess, we're going to have to get cleaners in."

Rosie stares at me, narrowing her eyes. "You look different."

I roll my eyes in an exaggerated motion before patting my hair down nervously. "I've just done the most embarrassing thing of my life, Rosie. Give me a break!" I laugh. "And maybe get me a drink!!"

She grins and nods, raising her hands slowly. "Alright, alright."

"Here," comes a deep voice behind me. I turn to see Zach, holding two glasses of wine. He hands me one and winks and suddenly I feel silly for being jealous of the barmaid. My head is spinning between the tree and the sex and just the overall thrill of being next to Zach for so long. Rosie is looking at me with her eyebrow raised so I bury my nose in my glass of wine and take a sip.

"Thanks," I say to Zach.

He nods his head and looks towards our coworkers. "I'd better go make the rounds. Glad you're feeling better."

His voice is different. It's more official now, the way it sounds when we're at work. I nod and he slips away.

"What was *that* about," Rosie breathes. I glance at her and she's looking at me, eyes shining bright as she searches my face. "What happened up there? I've never seen him buy a drink for anybody!"

"Rosie, stop," I say. "Can you just give me a break?! It's been a rough night." I try to laugh it off but it sounds forced even to me. Her eyebrow shoots up even higher and she smiles slightly.

"Rough night, hey?" She says pointedly. I stare at her until she grins. "Fine. But this conversation isn't over. I've known you long enough to know when you're hiding something from me."

I don't respond. I'd rather deal with the ridicule from my coworkers than Rosie's piercing stare. She's known me for years, and she can always tell when I've got something on my mind. I steal a glance towards Zach just as he looks up towards me. For a second our eyes meet and then he looks back towards the man he was talking to.

My heart is suddenly racing. I don't know what's going on! This isn't like me! I'm not the type to have casual sex, let alone casual sex *with my boss at the office Christmas party*! The way he looked at me just now sent a thrill straight through my chest. I can feel my heart pounding against my ribcage and suddenly I remember the way it felt to have his hands all over me and his cock buried deep inside me. I close my eyes and breathe in deeply, trying to remember the sensation of his body against mine.

Rosie clears her throat and my eyelids fly open. She's staring at me, her eyes searching mine. Suddenly her eyes widen and she takes a step back, her hand flying up to her chest and her jaw dropping to the floor. She takes a step towards me and leans in.

"You fucked him," she whispers forcefully. "You fucked him, didn't you!"

I can't say anything, I just feel the redness spreading over my cheeks. Rosie's eyes widen some more and she bursts out laughing.

"No!"

I shrug.

"*No!* Harper!"

"Oops?" I suggest as I start to chuckle. She grabs me by the elbow and guides me towards the corner of the room.

"Tell. Me. *Everything.*" She says into my ear as she leads me away from the crowd. "*Everything.*"

10

ZACH

I'M SCANNING the room for her and I can't see her. There's deep disappointment welling up inside me as I realise she's gone and I hate myself for it. Women don't have this effect on me! I'm the one who's in control! I glance back to my employees, a ring of three of them around me all vying for my attention. It's exhausting. Even Becca, my assistant who usually entertains me with a bit of a flirt seems so boring and vapid now. Her tight top just seems overdone. *She'd never pull off a light-up Christmas sweater from the thrift store.*

Shaking my head, I try to focus on what they're saying. This isn't like me. We slept together and that's it. She left the party without saying goodbye, so that says it all. It's better this way, anyways. People would talk if they saw us speaking to each other too much. It would just be more Christmas party rumours.

Still, I find myself wishing she was here. I keep looking around for her, wanting to see those eyes of hers.

It must be lust. That's the only explanation. She was so wild in bed—*ahem*, on the sofa—and I'm just wanting more.

Why else would I be looking for her like this? I'm just reeling from my orgasm is all. Nothing more.

"So you took care of Harper up there, hey," says a man's voice from behind me. I frown. He has a high-pitched voice and there's a hint of an edge to it. I turn around slowly and see a short balding man with a big beer belly. His beady black eyes are staring at me and I don't know if I'm imagining the fury burning in them. He blinks and his face loses all emotion. It's like he wilfully rearranges his features to hide something. Am I imagining things? I'm just as paranoid as Harper now!

"Yes, Harper is feeling better. She was lucky she didn't get injured when the tree fell," I respond, keeping my voice steady.

The man says nothing, just stares at me with those small black eyes. His hair is plastered to his forehead and he looks like he has a permanent sheen of sweat on his face. He stares at me so long it starts to get unnerving. What did he mean by 'take care of Harper?' Finally he speaks again.

"You seem to know her pretty well," he says, his voice flat and emotionless. I frown. He's staring at me like there's more to his words than he's letting on.

"I'm sorry I didn't catch your name?"

"Greg," he says slowly. "Greg Chesney. From accounts."

I nod and give my usual answer when I have no idea who one of my employees is. "Of course."

We stare at each other for a few moments and I'm scrambling to find something to say when without warning, he spins around and weaves his way through the crowd and disappears.

"What was that about?" Mitch asks as soon as the man walks away. I take a deep breath and turn towards him.

"I'm not sure. It was fucking weird though."

"Fucking nutcase if you ask me. Does he work for us??"

"That's Greg," says Becca. "He's a creep. He was totally stalking one of the women at the office last year, I don't know how he kept his job."

I glance at her and frown. Suddenly my heart is beating a little bit faster. "Stalking?!"

She nods her head. "Secret admirer kind of thing. She'd get letters delivered to her house and phone calls with just heavy breathing. I think he showed up at her house a couple times. So creepy."

"Who?" I almost shout. "Who was the woman? Why didn't I know about this!" My heart starts hammering in my chest and I remember the fear in Harper's eyes when she heard something outside, and the way she stared at those plastic plates. Was it her?? Did she have a *stalker* and then had to keep working with him for a year?! Why wouldn't someone fire the bastard!

Suddenly Becca seems uncomfortable. She wrings her hands. "I... I don't know. It's confidential, Mr. Lockwood. I'm not even supposed to know about it. HR handled it last year and I never heard the details. You could ask them?"

I stare at her for a few seconds, trying to see if she's telling the truth. Suddenly it looks like her face breaks and she brings her hands up in front of her.

"Please don't tell them I told you! They'll never forgive me for it. They could make my day a living hell."

I soften my look and shake my head. "Don't worry, Becca. Nothing is going to happen to you."

The room feels stuffy. I feel like I'm being smothered, like every breath is a struggle. I excuse myself and head for the door. I keep my head down and weave through the crowd in the bar, not pausing to talk to the people who call out my name. They all just want me to notice them, to move up the ladder in any small way they can.

I walk outside and the cold winter air hits me like a wall. There's snow falling lightly and I know it would be a beautiful winter evening if I didn't feel like I was suffocating. I catch a glimpse of Harper climbing into a cab with her friend Rosie. I watch as they drive away and I feel a punch in the gut. The taillights are bright in the dark night and I stand there until the car drives out of sight. She was serious, when she said it was a one-time thing. She left without saying goodbye.

I spin around and start stomping down the street in the other direction. Usually it's me who leaves the women hanging! How dare she just toss me aside like I'm some piece of meat! I stuff my hands into my pockets and try to walk off the frustration inside me. This isn't how the night was supposed to end! She was supposed to be mine! The cool winter air fills my lungs and calms me down as I walk away from the bar, away from the office, away from *her*.

After a few minutes I calm down. The anger that flared inside me subsides. I'm not mad, I'm just not used to meeting a woman who's so in control of herself. She's right to walk away from me, we need to keep it professional from now on. I need to keep my distance from her and my attraction to her will pass. Hopefully she keeps wearing those ugly sweaters and I can forget what she looks like underneath.

11

HARPER

"I DON'T KNOW what else to tell you, Rosie. It just sort of... happened."

"Harper, come on," Rosie says while looking at me sideways. "These things don't just happen. You slept with New York's most eligible bachelor! He's rich, he's handsome and he's *your boss*!! What are you going to do now?"

I shrug. "I'll just go to work on Monday and pretend it never happened."

As soon as the words leave my lips I know it's easier said than done. How can I pretend it never happened when I haven't been able to stop thinking about it all night?? I had to stop myself from staring at him, and even when I told Rosie what happened I could feel my body yearning for him. In the end I had to run away or I knew I would do something stupid.

Rosie shakes her head. "You're unbelievable. Only you could pull the Christmas tree down on top of you and then proceed to sleep with your boss an hour later." She laughs.

"Half an hour later," I correct.

Rosie laughs. "I'm so glad I met you. You make life interesting, if nothing else."

I grin. "I'm glad I can provide some entertainment for you."

The cab pulls up to my house.

"You sure you're okay, Harper? You don't want me to stay till tomorrow in case you need to go to the hospital? What if you have a concussion?"

"You're the best friend I could ask for, Rosie, but no, I'm fine. I just want to relax and sleep."

"Alright," she says, putting her arm out. We hug quickly and I get out of the cab and walk to my front door.

I see a movement out of the corner of my eye and glance over. Is someone there? Rosie's cab has already driven off and my street is uncomfortably silent. I peer into the darkness but I don't see anything. My heart starts beating a bit faster until I finally find my keys. Once I'm inside I rush up the stairs to my apartment, I turn on all the lights and lock the door. That's better. I shiver slightly and push the feeling away. It's just too much excitement for one evening. With a deep breath, I calm myself down and shake my head. My nerves are shot.

I start getting ready for bed. After a few drinks and all the excitement of the evening I feel absolutely exhausted. I brush my teeth and climb into my bed in record time, knowing that I'll be asleep as soon as my head hits the pillow.

That doesn't happen though. I get under the covers and immediately I feel wide awake. Suddenly my body feels cold, like it needs the feel of another person's skin against it. I try to close my eyes but as soon as I do, Zach's face paints itself on my eyelids. I see the way he looked at me when we were cleaning in the office, the way his eyes raked up my body and his desire was written all over his face.

I sigh, and let my hand drift down to my mound. Even the thought of him looking at me makes the wetness gather between my legs. I sigh as my hand starts working its way around my bud, gently at first and then faster. I remember the way his hands felt on my hips, on my ass, the way he kissed my nipples and pulled my head down towards his lips.

I remember the way my hips bucked as I rode him, almost as if by instinct. Our bodies moved together and every sound, every moan, every touch was electric. I imagine what it would be like to be with him now, if he were on top of me and our naked bodies were intertwined. I could run my hands over his broad chest and grab onto his shoulders as he thrusts his cock inside me. I could actually feel his skin against mine, we wouldn't have our clothes on like we did in his office. We could take our time. I could touch him and feel his body against mine, feel him push deeper and deeper inside me.

God, I want to feel that cock again. As my fingers twirl around my clit I just think of the way it felt to be filled up by him, to have him sheathed inside me as deep as he can go. I want to have him deep inside me again. I want to feel him come inside me like he did earlier.

The thought of him pumping his seed into me makes my walls contract and my wetness intensify. I can feel myself edging closer and closer to orgasm, and I just think about the way his eyes burned when he looked at me, and the way my skin sizzled with every touch. I think of the way his hands gripped me and pulled me down as his cock drove into me harder, faster, deeper.

I come at the thought of his orgasm pumping into me. I let my legs fall open and exhale as the pleasure washes over me. All too soon, it's over. I take a deep breath and open my eyes.

I came as I was thinking of his white seed spilling into me and the thought makes me blush, even alone in my own bed. I shouldn't want that, it shouldn't turn me on but it does.

That orgasm was nothing compared to the real thing. Maybe now I'll be able to sleep, but if anything it's only made me want him more. I fall asleep thinking of the way it felt to have him inside me.

I WAKE up with the cold December light streaming through my open blinds. It's not helping the headache that pounds in my skull. Too much wine.

As soon as my eyes open, I'm thinking of the same thing I fell asleep thinking about—Zachary Lockwood's cock buried deep inside me. It's a feeling I won't forget in a hurry.

I sigh and swing my legs off the edge of the bed. I'll have to forget it, because come Monday he'll be back to being my boss, and I'll be back to being his bumbling employee who ruined the Christmas party.

12

ZACH

"MORNING ZACH," Mitch says to me. "Good weekend? You didn't come out on Saturday! Great talent at the club," he winks. I try not to groan.

"Nah, wasn't feeling it." I try to slip past him without answering any more of his questions. He's a great friend but I'm not in the mood to hear about what girls were at which club and how many he took home this weekend. I can't deal with that today. It's been two weeks since the Christmas party and Mitch has been pestering me to go out almost every single night. I just can't muster up the energy.

The past few weeks have been the longest weeks of my life. For the first time in a long, long time I've actually been looking forward to going in to the office. I look forward to Mondays. I walk across the office and scan the room.

The cleaners did a good job with the mess from the Christmas tree incident and the place finally looks back to normal. Everyone else is either working or milling around like any other morning. I can't help but feel like something has shifted. There's a slight buzz in the room, it's the last week before the holiday break, but I know that's not what's changed.

I glance around the room but I already know what's different. I'm looking for her again, just like I have been every day for the past two weeks. I shake my head and walk into my office, closing the door behind me.

Usually, a couple weeks would see many women come and go in my life but I haven't even met a single one that interests me. I glance over at the couch and my thoughts flick back to that night. I think of Harper sitting on top of me and it feels like it happened yesterday. We were right there. That's where she was when she was riding me like her life depended on it and I had one of the best orgasms of my life. Even looking at the empty sofa makes my cock start to throb in my pants.

"Ahem," comes a soft voice behind me. I turn to see Becca. She's wearing some sort of semi-office appropriate low cut top and she's leaning down to give me the full view of her cleavage. She smiles coyly. "Morning Mr. Lockwood. I have a message for you from Mr. Latif." She hands me a piece of paper and then lingers. I glance at the paper then back at her.

"Anything else?" I ask dryly. She looks a bit taken aback. I open my mouth to say something nicer and then decide to close it again.

"No, no that's it." She pauses again. "Did you have a good weekend?"

"It was fine," I say as I open the paper, turning around without looking at her. I sit at my desk and finally look up. She's still here. "Becca, I'm still waiting for Greg Chesney's file. It's been over a week since I asked.

She nods. "HR wouldn't release the file right away. Confidentiality issues. I'll chase them up again."

"What kind of confidentiality stops the CEO of the company from accessing an employee file?!"

"I'm not sure, Mr. Lockwood. I'll chase them up again this morning."

I nod. She lingers, and I wave to the door. "Would you mind closing that on the way out?"

She nods again quietly and finally leaves. I sigh when the door clicks closed. That was painful. Our once flirty relationship has gotten very strained lately. I know it's me, I'm the one who's been acting different but I can't help it.

It doesn't matter. She'll just have to get used to it. Hopefully she'll have some useful information for me about Greg Chesney and I can find out who this guy is and why he still works for me.

I turn my eyes back to the note in my hand and read it again. I sigh, rubbing my temples. This is not good news. One of our biggest clients has just moved a deadline to the beginning of January, and the new timeline is almost unachievable. I glance at the calendar—the staff is supposed to be on holiday from Thursday this week until the New Year. We're going to have to work through Christmas. I pick up the phone and dial Becca's desk.

"Yes Mr. Lockwood?"

"Becca, get the management team in here. I need everyone as soon as possible."

"No problem," she says and I click the phone down. Might as well deliver the news right away and see who volunteers to work through the holidays.

It only takes a couple minutes for my management team to assemble. The first person to walk in is Harper. She looks right at me from across the room and immediately my cock jumps in my pants. I quickly shift my weight and say a silent thanks that I'm sitting down behind my desk.

Get a fucking grip!!

"Good weekend?" She says in that musical voice of hers. Why is everyone so interested in my weekend?!

"Yeah it was fine, relaxing," I respond. She nods and sits down on the sofa exactly where I was on that Friday night with her legs straddling my lap. She brushes an imaginary piece of dust off the sofa and glances at me through her eyelashes. My cock twitches again. I clear my throat.

"How was yours?"

"Same," she shrugs. She glances at me again but before I can speak, Mitch walks in.

"What's this about, Zach?" He says in that booming voice of his.

"Let's wait for the rest of the team to get here." Mitch nods and sits down on one of the chairs opposite my desk. It only takes a couple minutes for the dozen management executives to come in the door.

"Right, team, I've had some bad news. The Latifs have moved their deadline up to January 2nd. We will need to deliver the entire advertisement proposal to them by that day or else they'll pull out of the contract."

"*What?!*" Mitch exclaims. I hold up a hand.

"Before anyone protests, I'm volunteering to carry this through myself. We need a skeleton team to work through the holidays to get this done. I'll need one of you and about half a dozen team members. You'll get time off in lieu in January, after the project is delivered." I glance at my team and a heavy silence hangs on the room. "Any volunteers?"

I can see them glancing at each other, hoping someone else will put their hand up. How many of them have holidays and trips planned? How many of them will want to spend time with their families? I know I'm asking a lot, but I have no choice.

"I'll work," says a familiar voice from the sofa. I look over to see Harper staring directly at me. Her green eyes look like they're gleaming from within. "I don't have a family or plans for the holidays so I have the least to give up. I'll work."

We look at each other for a moment. I can't tell if she's doing this because I'll be here with her. As soon as the thought crosses my mind, I know she isn't. She's just dedicated to the job and she knows everyone else has kids and families to go back to. I nod.

"Thanks, Harper. I'll send you a full brief this morning. That's it, everyone. Thanks for coming in." I nod my head and everyone stands. They file out of my office one by one, the last one being Harper. She glances at me quickly and then turns to walk out. Her ass moves from side to side with every step and I watch her walk away until she turns the corner.

I don't know whether to be excited or worried about this. Somehow I feel both.

13

HARPER

WE ARE PROFESSIONALS. This is fine. I feel a wave of nausea come over me as I walk out of his office but I push it down.

Why would I volunteer?!

I should have just kept my mouth shut. I've been trying to avoid spending time with him, and now I'm going to be stuck in close quarters for almost two weeks! Is that why I said I'd do it? I can try to lie to myself and say it was because other people have families and holidays, but a part of me knows it's because of Zach. I see Rosie poke her head up from her cubicle and I walk over.

"What was that about?" She whispers. "Everyone was in his office."

"The Latif file. They've moved the deadline to January 2nd."

Rosie's eyes widen. "Can they do that?!"

I shrug. "Apparently. I'm working through Christmas."

"What!"

"Yeah, no one else was volunteering. It's not so bad, I'll take some time off in January to make up for it. I have to put a team together so if you want some overtime and great holiday memories just let me know." I know my voice sounds unusually cheery.

Rosie's eyes narrow. She searches my face and then her lips tug upwards. She sits back in her chair and crosses her arms with a triumphant grin.

"*He's* working, isn't he?"

"Who?" I ask innocently, even though I know who she means. She rolls her eyes.

"Zach!" She whispers. "I can see right through you, Harper, you are unbelievable!"

I grin and throw my hands up. "I'm a professional, Rosie. I'm just a slave to the job, is all."

"You're a slave to something," she says with an eyebrow raised. I laugh and walk away before someone hears us, or before Rosie makes me face things I'm not ready to think about.

Back in my office, I flop down on my chair and let out a sigh. Maybe Rosie is right, and I'm just doing this to be close to Zach. That's the last thing I need—to complicate this, this.. whatever this is. It's been hard enough to keep my distance since the party, and now it's about to get a whole lot harder.

I shake my head. Who am I kidding, of course I said I'd do it because of him. The second he said he was working through I knew I'd volunteer. It just took a couple seconds to work up the courage. I can tell myself I'm a professional, I can tell myself I care about the work, but in the end I know I said yes because I haven't stopped thinking about Zach since the night we slept together. I was sitting right where we had sex, right where we were when he was inside me. The past two weeks have just been one big daydream with a few self-love sessions featuring Zach and that big cock of his.

I close my eyes and try to push out the thought of him. When I said I'd volunteer he looked right at me. His gaze just pierced right through me and I could feel myself getting wet. If one look does that to me, how am I going to survive two weeks working side by side with him?! The last time I had a full conversation with him we ended up sleeping together in his office!

There's a knock on the door and it makes me jump up. My eyes fly open.

"Zach, hi!" I say, my voice just a little bit too forced. He walks in and closes the door behind him.

"Thanks for volunteering to work," he says in a low voice. "I know it's not easy to give up your holidays." I nod. My mouth is dry. He sits down across from me and places his hands down on the armrests. He's staring at my desk and it looks like he's trying to think of what to say. Finally he raises those deep brown eyes and looks right at me. He takes a deep breath and speaks again.

"I thought that since we'll be working together we should lay out some ground rules."

"Ground rules," I repeat slowly.

"Yeah, ground rules." His eyes flick down my body and then back up to my face and I feel my core heat up instantly. I try to keep myself from reacting, but my cheeks predictably start to flush. "What happened between us was.. unexpected. It was great! Don't get me wrong!"

He pauses, and I feel my lips twitch upwards into a smile.

"Zach, please," I start gently. He glances at me. "We're both adults. We had sex and it was fun, but now we need to work together. I understand that. I'm not looking for anything from you, or with you."

He takes a deep breath and nods. "Great. So we understand each other."

"We understand each other," I repeat. *I understand that you look incredibly sexy in that suit right now*. I take a deep breath and try to smile.

"You're an important part of this team, Harper. I wouldn't want anything to get in the way of that, and I wouldn't want you to feel uncomfortable."

There's a silence between us and I feel like he wants to say more, but nothing comes out. I turn to my computer screen.

"You'll send that information through today? I'll get a start on it as soon as I get it and come up with a plan of attack. I'll start getting a team together that can work with us."

He goes back to being the serious, stone-faced executive I knew last week. The moment between us has passed, and I feel both relieved and disappointed.

"That's great, Harper. Have a team list and program on my desk by the end of the day."

"Done."

He turns around and I watch the way his pants grip his ass with every step until the door closes and he's out of view. I slump back in my chair and let all the air out of my lungs.

This is fine.

I can do this.

This is definitely fine.

14

ZACH

"Hey Mitch, what can I do for you," I say as I walk back into my office. Mitch is sitting in his favourite seat across from my desk. This morning is exhausting already. Maybe I was wrong about looking forward to Mondays, so far this one is just one headache after another.

"Just wanted to check in. You've been acting weird this past little while."

"Weird?" I ask without meeting his eye. I flop down onto my chair and keep my eyes on my computer screen, pretending to type something.

"What happened?"

"When?" I'm trying to keep my voice as steady as possible. He knows me well enough to know when something is bothering me. My eyes flick to his. He's staring at me intently and I know he's trying to work out what's changed. Nothing has changed!

His eyes narrow. "Who is she?"

"What?!" I lean back in my chair and throw my hands up.

"Last time you were acting like this was when you and

your ex broke up. Have you been seeing someone and you didn't tell me?!"

"Mitch, you've spent almost every weekend with me except for the last one or two. If I had a girlfriend don't you think you'd know by now? Can't I have a weekend away from it all?" I shake my head. "You're fucking clingy, man."

Mitch laughs. "Alright, alright." He throws his hands up before standing up. "You want me to do anything for this Latif file?"

"Talk to Harper, see if she's got anything for you to do."

"Alright no problem. No complaints there," he smirks. "She's a fine piece of ass, hey. Something about her, you know?"

The anger flares up inside me and I feel my blood pumping like liquid heat through my veins. I almost lunge at Mitch the minute the words leave his mouth.

"Shut the fuck up, Mitch!" I exclaim, surprising myself with the force of my words.

Mitch looks taken aback. "Sorry, Zach," he says after a pause.

"She works with us. Come on." I bite my tongue. I don't want him to know about Harper and I. It's too different with her. It's not like my other hookups

Mitch frowns and I know he's thinking about other conversations we've had about women. I've never reacted like this. I can't help it, hearing him say those things about Harper makes the anger spark inside me. I stare at him until he turns around slowly and walks out without saying anything. As soon as he's gone I let out a sigh. What the fuck is wrong with me?!

I know the answer to that. It's Harper. She's gotten under my skin. All it took was one night. Not even one night! Part of one night and now I'm useless. I can't look at another woman and she won't even give me the time of day.

My pulse is still elevated. I hated hearing him talk like that. He was so fucking crass! About a woman like Harper, who is his better in so many ways!

This would be a lot easier if she didn't look so goddamn good all the time. I don't even know what it is about her! I have been with supermodels, actresses, singers, whoever I wanted! But she's got a realness, or an earthiness, or *something* that gives her this irresistibleness. Mitch has seen it, obviously. It's like I can tell there's more to her than meets the eye. I mean, I know there is, I experienced that other side of her the night of the Christmas party.

I lean back in my chair and rub my temples. I shouldn't have reacted like that. I know that he annoyed me because he's right. I haven't been myself for weeks. I glance at the couch again. I can still see her pulling her pants down and sitting right onto my cock as if she was right in front of me again. I can still see that look in her eye when she came on top of me.

She's so unbelievably sexy. Even just now I could barely keep my eyes off her body, and she was the perfect professional. Maybe it was just sex for her. It must have been.

I haven't been this attracted to a woman since my ex. I don't even know if I was this attracted to my ex, or anyone, ever! It feels different with Harper. She's got me off-balance and I'm not sure I like it. I want more of her, and wanting it scares me. She's exactly the type of woman that I've always stayed away from.

I should just stick to the women who want money and status. It's easier that way, all that emotion and complication isn't worth it. I know it, Mitch knows it, even Harper knows that it's not worth it. I just have to keep telling myself that.

It's not worth it.

It's not worth it.

It's not worth it.

Maybe if I say it enough I'll start to believe it.

15

HARPER

"THAT'S VERY GENEROUS, Greg, but the team has filled up now. You enjoy your holiday," I say to Greg as he shifts his weight from foot to foot in front of me. He's got his hands in his pockets and his greasy hair is plastered to his forehead as usual. He licks his lips.

"Are you sure? Wouldn't it be better to have more hands on deck? I don't have holiday plans and I know that other people do. I don't mind spending the holidays here with you... and the team."

Even his voice sends an uncomfortable feeling crawling down my spine. I force a smile.

"Thanks Greg, I'll look into it. At the moment we won't need you to come in but I'll keep you in mind."

"Okay, thanks Harper. Is there anything I can do in the meantime? To help?"

"No, that's fine, I'm sure you have a lot on your plate to finish up before the break. Thanks Greg."

I turn to my screen as if to say, *we're done now, you can leave.* I can feel his eyes on me and it makes me want to shudder. I don't know what it is about him that makes me so uncomfortable. I think it's the way he stares at me always a second too long, or the way he always seems to pop up around the corner when I least expect him. I never feel at ease around him.

I never found out if it was him who called me and just breathed over the phone, or if he was the one who left notes in my mailbox. The only thing I was able to prove was that he was lurking outside my house and according to HR that was only grounds for a warning. Everything stopped after the warning though: the phone calls, the notes, the prickly feeling at the back of my neck.

He leaves my office and I let out a sigh, glancing through the glass to make sure he walks away. Maybe that feeling is just leftover nausea from this morning. I don't know what's been wrong with me these past few days, but I wake up feeling like I'm going to throw up. Even the smell of coffee when I first get up makes me want to vomit, and I drink coffee like it's water.

It might not be Greg that makes me feel uneasy at all, it's whatever this stomach bug is that I have. I rub my temples and feel uncomfortable tightness around my favourite ring. I slip it off my finger and place it into the top drawer. Between Greg, the nausea and feeling like my fingers are little sausages this whole day is just uncomfortable.

I look down at my organisation chart and I know we have gaps for the holiday work period. We could definitely use another body to get us to meet this deadline, but I just can't say yes to Greg. The thought of spending two weeks with him in a half-empty office with long nights and lots of overtime just sounds like a recipe for disaster. If it means I have to put in more hours myself then that's what I'll do.

I sigh and get up from my chair. Suddenly I need a coffee, or a snack, or *something*. Monday morning never seemed so long.

Once in the kitchen I grab a mug and grab the hot pot of coffee. Someone's just made a fresh pot and I silently thank them, whoever they are. As soon as I grab the pot the smell of the coffee me hits like a wall and I feel a wave of nausea come over me. I put the pot back down and grab onto the counter.

Rosie's voice makes me jump.

"Harper, are you okay? What just happened?" she whispers furtively.

I turn and see her standing in the doorway wearing a worried expression on her face. I frown, trying to force a weak smile as my stomach quiets down again.

"What do you mean?" I answer. "I'm fine."

"You look like you're about to hurl," she whispers again with a frown. "Is it because of Greg?" She takes a few steps towards me. My heart starts beating faster. I try to keep my voice steady.

"What about him?"

"He left your office and he looked like he was about to punch through the wall! I've never seen him look that angry! I mean, except for the time I confronted him about following you."

My heart is thumping in my chest. It's not right to feel this uncomfortable at work! I turn to Rosie and she places her hand on my arm.

"Harper, is everything okay? Do you want me to talk to him?"

"No!" I exclaim. "Thanks Rosie, but last time it made such a scene, I don't want to put you in that position again. Not for my sake."

"I don't mind. I'll slap the fucker if I have to." Her eyes are blazing. Last year I never would have had the strength to approach HR if Rosie hadn't supported me.

I shake my head. "It's nothing. He asked to be on the Latif team. I said no," I reply. "I lied to him, we do need more people to volunteer. Maybe he knows that."

Her face contorts with worry. "It didn't look like he took it well. Look, I'll work. Would that help?"

I smile. "That would help a lot, actually. Are you sure?"

She nods and I take a deep breath before turning back to the pot of coffee. The smell is still overwhelming and nauseating. I don't know what to say.

If Greg was mad, that's bad news for me. I try not to think of those months last year when I was consumed with fear and paranoia. I've convinced myself there's no need to worry, but Rosie's face says it all.

"What am I supposed to do, Rosie?" I ask as I turn back to her. I shrug and plead with her with my eyes. There are a thousand unsaid things weighing on me but with one look I know she understands.

"We'll figure it out together," she responds, straightening her back. I see her resolve strengthen and the fear leave her eyes. "Record everything about the conversation. I'll write down what I saw. If he causes any issues we'll have everything on paper."

I nod. "Okay."

My thoughts fly back to that Friday night two weeks ago at the Christmas party, to the stack of plates on the floor. The nagging feeling comes back to me like a wave.

"Rosie," I start. I don't even know what to say. "The Christmas party..."

"What about it?" She takes a step towards me. I glance

around to make sure no one is within earshot and I lower my voice.

"I think someone was here, you know, while we were..."

Rosie's eyes widen and she takes another step towards me. She's a couple inches taller than me and she bends her head closer to mine.

"You think it was Greg?"

"I don't know!" I exclaim, shrugging my shoulders. "I don't know! There could have been no one here."

"Why do you think there was someone here?"

I take a deep breath. Suddenly it seems silly to think that a stack of plastic plates would mean that someone saw me with Zach. I force myself to say it out loud to Rosie, who's staring at me intently. Maybe if I say it, the nagging fear that we were seen will go away.

"We were in his office and I heard something. Like a noise or a bang or something out in the main room. Zach went out and didn't see anyone and then we... you know." I look around again and whisper. "*Slept together.*"

"Right," Rosie says with a grin. "You told me about that part already."

I can't help but smile. My smile fades as I tell her the next part. "When we were leaving I saw a stack of plates on the ground. I *know* I put them on the table. I remember putting them on table! But then when we left they were on the floor. But you know, the place was a mess so I could be wrong. It was a disaster with food and cutlery and decorations everywhere. We were fooling around near the table and they could have fallen off, but I *swear* I remember them being on the table! I'm probably wrong, but I don't know, Rosie, I just have this feeling."

"Like someone knocked them over and that's what you heard?"

"Yes!" I exclaim. I inhale deeply and Rosie puts her hand on my forearm.

"Maybe. But let's not panic," Rosie says gently. "It's possible someone was here, and it is possible it was Greg." I shiver, and Rosie continues. "*But*, it's also possible that you were all hopped up on wine and endorphins and your sex-addled mind was hearing things and thinking things. I mean, at the end of the day you slept with Zach Lockwood *at the office!* Who knows what kind of tricks your mind would play on you in that situation!!"

I chuckle. "I definitely wasn't thinking straight."

"So let's not panic, okay? Let's just write everything down and if things get weird with Greg we'll have some backup. We can operate on the assumption that no one knows about Friday night except you and me." She pauses and cocks her head to the side. "And Zach, obviously."

I grin. "Oh right, him."

"Did I mention how generous it was of you to spend all that overtime locked up in this office with him over the next few weeks? What a sacrifice you're making for the team."

"Shut up, Rosie," I laugh. "You'd do the same."

"I'd do worse," she replies with a laugh. I giggle and then sigh. Rosie gives my shoulders a squeeze and I sigh again. I feel better.

"Thank you," I say softly.

"You know I'd do anything for you, right?"

I smile. "I wouldn't have made it through the past year without you."

With one more squeeze of my shoulders she winks at me and we head back to our desks.

16

ZACH

I'M LOOKING at the HR report on Greg Chalmers and I can feel my blood boiling. Why wasn't I told about this?! The woman's name is censored from the report and I wish I knew who it was. I'm told she still works here, and I can't imagine how uncomfortable it must be for her.

I read through the details of the file. I can't believe this guy still works for us. He followed and harassed a coworker for *months*. I read through the transcript of a meeting with her and I shiver.

I'm always looking over my shoulder, I don't feel safe. He was outside my house!

The HR representative asked her if she wanted to press charges and she said no. Why would she say no? She had grounds to get this guy fired and she never pursued it. Why??

At the moment we don't have enough evidence to fire him. A 'feeling' isn't evidence, you understand that, right Ms Anderson?

I can almost hear the contempt in this person's voice, even just reading the transcript. How are they not outraged?! This must have been incredibly difficult for whoever was sitting on the other side of the table.

I push my chair back and stand up. This has gone too far. If she wouldn't press charges then I will. I need to confront this guy directly. I feel like a fool! How did I not know this was going on?! I should know everything that happens in my company.

My hands fly up to my temples for the thousandth time this morning. I can't ignore the shame and disappointment that's making my stomach burn right now. The last year I've been neglecting my work. I've been too busy going out and meeting women, partying, or 'networking' as I call it. It's a necessary part of the advertising industry, but now I realise I've been neglecting my company, my employees! This was going on right under my nose as I was off having nice lunches and dinners and going out with a new woman on my arm every night. It's not right.

I stomp out of my office and turn the corner towards the accounting department. I can feel the anger flaring up deep inside me, giving every step a new purpose. No one is allowed to make my employees feel uncomfortable! No one! He followed her *to her house*!!

As soon as I'm done with him I'll find out who she is and apologise to her personally. I should have known. I should have been here.

I get to the maze of cubicles in the accounting department and turn to the first one.

"Where does Greg Chesney sit?" I ask gruffly. The middle-aged man looks up and shock paints itself on his face.

"Mr. Lockwood! Hi! Um, Greg? Greg sits over there." He points to a cubicle a couple work stations down.

"Thanks," I grunt. I march over to the cubicle and get

ready to chew his ear out. He'll feel the wrath of Zachary Lockwood. I take a deep breath and get ready to spit my words out.

One more step and I'm there.

And... No one. He's gone.

His desk looks perfectly clean and tidy, like he hardly has any work in progress. There aren't any personal effects. No photos, no plants, nothing hanging on the cubicle walls. Just a neat row of pencils and a stack of files with ordered tabs separating them.

I turn to the woman who sits next to him. Was she his victim? I don't even know her name. I've been a terrible boss.

"Where's Greg Chesney?"

She's wearing the same surprised expression as the last man. I guess I haven't been over here in a long while. Maybe ever.

"He's gone," she says quickly. "He was just here maybe an hour ago and he grabbed his bag and walked out. I asked him where he was going but he didn't even look at me."

The frustration inside me builds. This shouldn't be this hard!! I'm the CEO of this company! I built it from the ground up and I should be able to find one accountant when I need to speak to him!

I stalk back to my office with a dark cloud over my head.

"Becca!" I bark. She jumps and looks at me like a deer in the headlights. "Get Greg Chesney on the phone. I need to see him right away."

She nods and picks up the phone, finding his number and punching it in. I walk into my office and wait for her to page me through.

I'm taking deep breaths and composing my speech for him when she walks into my office.

"I couldn't get a hold of him, Mr. Lockwood," she says, wringing her hands with worry. "The number he gave us for his personal phone was disconnected. I tried his building but they said no one by that name lives there."

My heart starts thumping. "What?"

"I don't know," she says. Her mouth opens and closes again and she looks at me, terrified.

"Get HR on it. Do we not know anything about this guy?! Get him in here ASAP."

She nods and almost runs out the door.

"Becca," I call after her. She turns around. "Thanks for your help with this," I say. Her face softens and she nods before leaving my office. I lean back in my chair and rub my temples, closing my eyes and taking deep breaths. Rage won't help me, frustration won't help me. There could be a simple explanation for all this. I need to figure out what I'm going to ask this guy, who he is, how he got a job with us when we know virtually nothing about him.

I can't believe I've let this happen.

17

HARPER

THE DAYS ARE FLYING by this week. It's already Wednesday and I feel like I haven't looked up from my desk. Most of the office will be on vacation from tomorrow onwards but I'll be staying in. I look at the team list of people scheduled to work overtime with me. It's pathetically short. We can't force people to work over Christmas, and it looks like most people have lives of families. Lucky them.

"Harper," Rosie says quickly as she slips into my office. Her eyes are wide and I can tell she's about to tell me some juicy office gossip. She looks at me and her expression changes to bemused amusement. "Harper are you eating pickles at 8:30am?"

"What's wrong with that?!" I say before crunching into my fourth pickle of the day.

"That's disgusting," she says with a laugh.

"These are the best fucking pickles I've ever tasted in my life," I reply as I bite down. I don't know why I'm eating pickles at 8:30 but I had this almost insatiable craving for them and I had to stop at a grocery store on the way in to work. And you know what? I'm an adult. I'll eat pickles whenever I want to eat pickles. If that means 8:30am on a Wednesday morning in December, so be it.

Rosie shakes her head. "Whatever. Did you hear about Greg Chesney?"

Even his name makes me feel uncomfortable. I'm thoroughly sick of talking about him.

"No, what about him?"

"Apparently on Monday morning he took his stuff and left and he hasn't been back in the office since. HR had a fake phone and address so no one knows where he is! He's just fallen off the face of the earth."

I can feel the blood draining from my face. For once I'm not blushing. My heart starts beating hard and it feels like my chest is hollow. My eyes struggle to focus as I process what Rosie's just told me.

"What do you mean, fake address and phone number?"

"I mean, we have no idea where this guy is. The information we have on him is all bogus. They've been looking for him and he's just... gone!"

"Since Monday?"

"Since Monday!"

"What time on Monday?" I ask. I think about my conversation with him, and how angry he was afterwards. What if he left after speaking to me and being turned down from the holiday team? My blood runs cold as I think of Greg Chesney being angry at me. I have no idea what he's capable of.

"I don't know what time he left. In the morning." Rosie pauses. "Harper, I think that you should come stay at my place." I glance up at her and see the deep concern in her eyes. "If you want," she adds. "I... I don't know. I don't have a good feeling about this."

I look down at my desk and take a deep breath. If Rosie doesn't have a good feeling about it then I know I should be worried.

I almost say yes to Rosie right away, but then something happens inside me. I take a deep breath and think about the past year of my life. I feel a deep anger well up inside. It's not anger, not exactly. It's outrage. I look up at Rosie and I know that I have fire in my eyes.

"You know what? Fuck him. I'm *done* letting him control my life. Good fucking riddance. If he wants to walk out on this job then be my guest. I'm not going to rearrange my entire life because he's a fucking creep and no one would listen to me about it. I'm *done* being scared. I'm *done* being paranoid and looking over my shoulder!"

I'm shaking. I take a few ragged breaths and Rosie stares at me. Her eyes soften and I feel a tear fall onto my cheek. I'm crying. God I hate when I cry! Anytime I get angry or offended I start crying!! I wipe at the tears angrily and look at Rosie again. She's wringing her hands and her face is full of worry.

"Thank you, Rosie. Honestly. You're the best friend I've ever had. But I have to be able to stand on my own two feet. I can't let this guy control my life anymore!"

She nods and sits down across from me, reaching her hands across my desk. She grabs my hand in both of hers and looks me right in the eye.

"I get that and I admire you for it. I just want you to be safe."

I nod. "I'll be fine. I have pepper spray," I grin. She's the one who bought it for me last year.

Rosie laughs. "Good. Remember to spray downwind."

She stands up and walks out of my office. I take a deep

breath and wipe my eyes. I won't cry over this, not again. If Greg Chesney walked out and never came back, it should be a good thing. I won't let fear control my life, not anymore.

I look at the short list of names in front of me and take a deep breath. If that's all the people that are working, then so be it. I'll work longer hours starting today. Nothing will stand in the way of me delivering this project, not deadlines or holidays or understaffed teams. And definitely, definitely not Greg Fucking Chesney.

18

ZACH

I FLICK off the lights to my office and close the door as I walk out. Everyone is gone and the office is deathly quiet. I let all the air out of my lungs. It's going to be a long couple of weeks. As I cross the big room towards the elevators I see one light still on.

Harper's office. Her door is open.

I change my direction and knock on her door frame. She looks up and I remember what it's like to stare into her green eyes. It sends a thrill straight between my legs.

"You're here late," I say.

"So are you," she shoots back with a grin.

"Slave to the job," I reply as I walk in and take a seat across from her. "Surely you have better things to do than to stay here?"

"Just finishing up a couple things. I want to be able to hit the ground running tomorrow with the team. I've put together a program and I actually think the January deadline is achievable. It'll be tight, but it's doable."

I make a sound in response but truthfully, I'm not

listening to a word she's saying. I'm watching the way her dark hair frames her face and makes her skin looks like porcelain, and the way her eyebrows knot together slightly as she looks at her computer screen. She turns it towards me.

"Here, look," she says, pointing to the screen. I clear my throat and sit up, looking at the schedule she's put together. My eyes shoot up as I look at the work she's put into this. She's incredibly smart.

"That's clever," I say, pointing to her logic on the screen. "Good work."

"Thanks," she says simply. She doesn't seem flattered or flustered by my praise, it's almost like she didn't hear it at all. I watch as her chest rises and falls when she takes a deep breath and then she glances at me with those emerald eyes again.

"I think it's time for me to go home," she says with a smile. "Come back fresh again tomorrow."

"Thanks for volunteering to work, Harper. You're a huge part of the team."

She smiles sadly. "I appreciate that, Zach. There were definitely times when I felt like my voice wasn't being heard. It's better now. It's good to hear that from you."

I frown. "What do you mean?"

"Oh, nothing," she says, waving her hand and getting up. She grabs her bag and starts packing her things into it.

"Did you know Greg Chesney?" I ask suddenly. I stare at her, looking for any sign that she was his victim. I'm studying her and I can feel my body go rigid even from a few feet away. If he threatened her I swear I could wring his neck right now.

I watch as she freezes, her hand perched in mid-air above her purse. After a second she keeps moving but she never looks at me.

"I used to work with him when I was still in accounts, why?"

"He's disappeared."

"I heard," she says, finally looking at me. "Listen, I don't mean to be rude, but I really don't feel like talking about Greg Chesney right now. He gets way too much airtime already."

I laugh. I can't help it. She speaks her mind and she doesn't let anyone push her around. The thought makes me relax. I can't imagine Harper being the victim of a stalker, she's too strong. Surely it wasn't her. I stand up.

"Let me walk you to your car," I say.

"Oh, I take the subway to work," she replies, smiling. "The environment and all that."

"Well then let me drive you home."

"You don't need to go out of your way. It's fine, really."

"Please," I tell her. "It's no problem at all."

"I... alright. Thanks, Zach." She smiles at me and I try to ignore the throbbing in my cock. I don't know if her smile is friendly or professional. I don't know if she's accepting because it's convenient or because she wants to spend more time with me.

Honestly, I don't care either way. Harper is a mystery to me. I never know what she's going to say or do, if she's going to come up with a brilliant business plan or pull down the sixteen-foot office Christmas tree on top of her.

"You're a very interesting person, you know that Harper?"

She glances at me sideways. "Interesting how?" she asks with a grin. "That doesn't sound quite like a compliment." Her grin widens. "You're pretty interesting yourself."

"That didn't sound quite like a compliment either," I laugh. I resist the urge to put my hand on the small of her back when she walks out of her office beside me. Every part of me is screaming to touch her, to get closer to her, but I keep a healthy, professional distance. She was clear that she thought sleeping with me was a mistake and it was definitely a one time thing. She's right, anyways. We work together.

But that doesn't mean I can't just steal one glimpse of her ass in that pencil skirt, does it?

19

HARPER

"This is me," I say as he pulls over in front of my apartment. "Thanks for the lift."

"No worries," he says as he puts the car in park. I turn to look at him and the breath is almost knocked out of my body when I see his dark brown eyes. Maybe it's the dim light of the car, or maybe it's my own imagination but I see the same look that I saw on Friday night.

Desire.

We're silent for a second. I can't look away. All I can hear is the roar of my heartbeat in my ears. My mouth goes dry and my eyes flick to his lips as they part slightly. He's not moving, one hand on the stick shift and one hand on the steering wheel but he's looking right at me, right through me.

I want him. I could invite him up to my apartment and in moments he'd be inside me like he was that night three weeks ago. We could have another night together and I could finally feel what I've been dreaming of ever since the office Christmas party. I could lean over and kiss him right now, and I know he'd have his arms around me in an instant.

"I'll see you tomorrow," I hear myself saying. "Thanks again!"

And just like that, I look away and almost run out of the car. I fumble with my keys. There's a movement in the corner of my eye, someone walking out from the alley beside me but I ignore it. I finally get the key into the lock and rush into my apartment without looking back, my heart still beating against my ribcage. I lock myself into my apartment and lean against the door, closing my eyes and breathing heavily.

That took all my willpower. Every single ounce of it.

It's better this way, of course it is. It would be so incredibly inappropriate to invite him in. We're about to go into a two-week frenzy of work. I can't be distracted by the thoughts of his lips, or his hands, or his cock...

I shiver before turning on the heat in my apartment. I know my bed will be cold and I'll wake up huddled in one corner of it. I wonder what it would feel like to wake up in Zach's arms? To feel the warmth of his body against mine all night?

With a deep breath I drop my bags and take off my jacket. I need to stop this. I head to the kitchen and groan when I open my fridge door. Nothing looks appetising. I open the freezer and see a tub of ice cream.

Why not?

Looks like it's just me, myself, and ice cream tonight.

I WAKE up and practically have to sprint to the toilet bowl. I cough and dry heave and finally throw up some bile as the waves of nausea crash over me. Finally, the feeling subsides and I sit down on the ground, my hand still resting on the toilet. I take a deep breath and lift myself up, running the sink to rinse out my mouth. I hate this feeling. I'm going to need to go to the doctor, this is getting ridiculous. Aren't stomach bugs supposed to be done in a day or two? It's been almost a week!

I sigh and get ready for work. I take a bit more time than usual to make sure my makeup looks nice, and I wear my favourite skirt. I pause before I grab the matching blazer, seeing my red light-up Christmas sweater hanging in the closet next to it.

If everyone else is going to be off work for the holidays, I'm going to make my own holiday. I slip the sweater on over my top and flick on the lights. The tree on my chest starts flickering and I smile to myself. I check myself out in the mirror—tight pencil skirt and ugly sweater.

Perfect.

THE TEAM IS ALREADY ASSEMBLED by the time I get into the office. I take off my jacket and hear some laughter.

"Planning on pulling down some more trees, there, Harper?" Rosie calls out as she points to my sweater. "We got rid of the last one but I'm sure I can find one for you to topple over. In fact, I think there's one in the Rockefeller Center that's what, 100 feet tall?"

I twirl around for her and she laughs. Another voice joins hers and I spin back around to see Zach standing in his office door.

"I always liked that sweater on you, Harper," he says with a smile playing in his eyes. My cheeks flush immediately and Rosie's eyebrows shoot up towards her hairline. She gives me a knowing look and turns back towards her desk.

"It's the holidays, isn't it?" I respond, ignoring the flood of desire soaking through my panties. If he keeps looking at me like that I'm going to go absolutely crazy this week. I thought this sweater would be a deterrent!

I try to hide my embarrassment and my arousal by turning to my office and dropping my bag down. It seems like an instant later he's in my doorway.

"Did you wear that on purpose?" He says in a low growl, taking a few steps towards me.

"On purpose? I mean, yes? I didn't get dressed in the dark."

"No, Harper," he says, now inches away from me. I back up so that my thighs hit my desk and his chest is almost touching mine. "Did you wear that because you knew it would drive me wild."

If my heart wasn't thumping so hard I would burst out laughing. This is probably the least sexy item of clothing I own.

"I... no. Does it drive you wild?" My voice is trembling and my fingers are desperate to hook themselves around his neck. I watch as he licks his lips and his eyes flick back up to mine. He hesitates for a moment and then spins around and rushes out of my office. I watch as he runs his fingers through his perfectly styled hair and heads back to his own office, closing the door behind him.

All the air leaves my lungs and I sit down on the edge of my desk. I look out the door and I see Rosie, staring in with an eyebrow raised. She grins and shakes her head slowly in mock disapproval. I roll my eyes and turn around, still trying to catch my breath and slow down my heartbeat.

I should have brought a change of underwear.

20

ZACH

I DON'T EVEN THINK it would matter what she wears. I can't get her out of my head. When she took off her jacket and I saw that hideous sweater all I could think of was her legs straddling me in my office as she bounced up and down on my cock. Instant boner.

My office door is closed and I put my head in my hands. I shouldn't have gone to her, but it's like something I can't control. I've been trying to avoid her for the past two weeks but now we'll be here, working on the same project together day-in, day-out. It's almost too much to bear.

There's a knock on the door and Becca pokes her head in. She's almost stopped flirting with me now, which honestly is a bit of a relief. I nod my head and she slips in, holding a box in front of her.

"This came for you," she says as she places it down on my desk.

"Thanks Becca," I tell her. My voice softens. "And thanks for offering to work during the holidays. I know it isn't easy."

She nods and smiles shyly but says nothing before

turning around and slipping out the door. I need to be nicer to my employees, and actually know what's going on with them. I've spent too much time being the hot shot CEO. Where has that gotten me? Relieved that I have to work over the holidays so I don't spend them alone?

Maybe this project is my chance to change. I can get to know this small team, and actually make an effort to see them as people and not just as employees. I always thought Harper was cold and distant and professional, but when I see her interacting with the rest of the team I see another side of her that she never showed me before. Or maybe I never bothered to notice.

Everyone loves her. She's warm and funny and has an infectious laugh. People *want* to work for her. I see the way she asks more from her team and they push themselves because of it. She's a fantastic manager.

Here I am thinking of her as an employee again. She's not only a fantastic manager, it looks like she has real empathy, real connections with the team. She put together a great team of our best people to work over the holidays. I'm her boss but I doubt I could have convinced all of them to work. They *like* her. I wonder how many of them, if any, actually like me?

I sigh and grab the box that Becca left on my desk. Maybe I can learn something from Harper over the next few weeks. Or maybe this is just me giving myself permission to talk to her and hear that musical laugh of hers.

I rip the box open and find a small ring. It's silver, with thin winding strands. It looks very old and worn. There's a note underneath and as soon as I read it my blood runs cold.

Stay away from her.

There's nothing on the other side of the paper, just those four words, handwritten on a scrap of paper. My heart is pounding in my ears. I flip the box over and empty the contents, looking through the packaging for anything else. There's nothing. My breath is shallow and my mouth feels dry as I look at the empty box, the note, and the ring.

Stay away from her? From who?? I look at the ring more closely, try to see some engraving, anything that would give me a hint of whose it is.

Who the hell am I supposed to stay away from?? Who would threaten me? I flip the piece of paper over again and frown. This is so fucking weird. I haven't even spent any time with a woman! Not since Harper. I sit back in my chair and feel my eyebrows raise.

This is the longest I've gone without sleeping with someone in... I don't even know how long. The past few weeks I've just lost interest in chasing women and having casual sex. What's the point in it all? And *now* I get this message? When I'm on my own?

I stare at the box again and rack my brain. Who would be threatening me? Is this even a threat? I slip the ring and the note into my breast pocket right as my door swings open. I glance up and meet Harper's eyes.

"Just about to start the morning brief, if you wanted to join?"

"Be right out," I reply in my best business voice. She nods and closes the door. I exhale loudly. Even one look from her makes my body buzz, how am I supposed to make it through the next two weeks?!

I put the box and the packaging on a shelf behind me and get ready to join the rest of the team. I'll deal with the ring and the note later.

Before I know it, one day turns into the next and it's Friday evening again and almost everyone has gone home. I know I'll have to come in to work tomorrow but maybe it can be a short day. I finally click shut down on my computer and start gathering my things. My left hand moves to touch my right ring finger, where I always wore my grandmother's ring. My heart skips a beat when I don't feel it there, and then I remember I took it off at the beginning of the week.

It should be right here, in the top drawer. I pull the drawer open and frown. There's a few pens and bits of stationary but no ring. I empty the contents of the drawer but can't find it anywhere. I pull open the second drawer, then the third, starting to feel the familiar hollowness in my stomach when I've lost something.

I can't lose this ring! It was my grandmother's ring, and I've worn it every day since the day she gave it to me. I go through every drawer, move everything around on my desk, check and re-check my purse.

"Fuck," I breathe to myself as I slump down in my chair.

All of a sudden I'm exhausted and I feel the tears start to well up in my eyes. Why am I so fucking emotional right now?! I'm either horny or crying or laughing hysterically these days. I look at the calendar on my desk and frown. I'm late for my period, so maybe it's about to start and that's why I feel like this. I'll find the ring, but I can't handle being an emotional wreck.

A thought creeps into the back of my mind. Maybe the reason I haven't gotten my period is.... Could I be pregnant? All the cravings, the nausea?

I shake my head. It couldn't be. I've been tested. One in ten million chance, the doctor said. Almost completely infertile. *Almost.* I sigh and shake my head again. I wasted enough energy hoping for that one in ten million, I'm not going down that path again. I'm just PMSing, that's all.

I remember the way the doctor said those words. It felt like he reached inside me and tore my uterus out himself. Now the tears aren't just welling up in my eyes, they're pouring down my cheeks. I close my eyes and try to stop myself but I can't stop my ragged breaths.

"Harper, are you okay?" Zach's voice pierces through my sadness. My eyes fly open and I quickly brush the tears away. They're still falling out of my eyes and I hate myself for it. I sit up.

"Fine, fine. I'm fine. Sorry," I say, turning away from him. He walks into my office and comes around the desk, kneeling beside me.

"What's wrong? Are you okay? What happened?"

I look at him and see what looks like real concern in his face. He's staring at me so earnestly, so openly. He's kneeling beside me and every party of my body is screaming for me to reach over and touch him.

"Nothing happened," I say, brushing the last of my tears away. "God, this is so embarrassing."

"Stop, it's fine." He stands up and leans on the desk beside me. He's so close I can feel the heat of his body next to me. "It's been a stressful week."

"Yeah," I reply lamely. How could I explain why to my boss I was crying, no, *sobbing* in my office on my own. Because I lost a ring? Because three years ago I was told I would never have children?? How completely pathetic of me.

"Harper, if this is about work, you should take the weekend off. You've put together a brilliant plan and the team will be able to carry it through."

He's staring at me again with those eyes. His face looks softer than it usually does, and his voice is barely louder than a whisper. It almost sounds like he really cares. I shake my head.

"I've got a couple things to do tomorrow. Don't worry about me, Zach, you just caught me at a bad time. I don't know what's wrong with me."

"There's absolutely nothing wrong with you, Harper."

Something in the way he says it makes my eyes flick up towards him. The softness in his eyes makes my heart grow twice its size and a soft warmth floods my veins. Zach reaches over and runs his finger along my temple, then tucks a strand of hair behind my ear. I close my eyes and inhale deeply as his finger traces the line of my jaw.

For the first time in three weeks, I ignore the voice that's telling me this is wrong. All I've wanted is to feel his touch, and now he's here next to me and everything feels *right*. My hand moves up to meet his and he grabs it, pulling me up to face him. He's still leaning on my desk and suddenly I'm standing in front of him. He pulls me into him and wraps his arms around me, then brings his hand up to my cheek to wipe away the last of my tears.

"Don't cry," he says softly.

"I'm not crying," I reply. "Not anymore, anyways."

"Good," he grins.

Time stands still as our faces move towards each other. I can feel the heat of his thighs on either side of my body and the warmth of his hand on my lower back. His other hand cups my face and then tangles into my hair as he brings my head closer to his. Finally, *finally*, our lips crush together and I taste his kiss again.

He tastes better than I remember. My arms hook themselves around his neck and I lean into him, pressing myself against his broad chest as his arms pull me in even closer. We kiss and kiss and kiss until I have to pull away to catch my breath.

"Let's get out of here," he growls. "I've been dreaming about you for three weeks, Harper. Come home with me."

"Okay," I reply. It's the only response I can manage, even though I want to tell him that I've been dreaming of him too. I want to tell him that every orgasm I've given myself these past few weeks I've been thinking of him, and every time I see him all I want to do is run my fingers all over his body.

I don't say any of that. I can't. My throat feels tight and all I can do is stare at him, wide-eyed with my heart thumping against my ribs. He kisses my lips one more time and then grabs my hand. I pick up my purse and we head out the door together.

22

ZACH

MY BODY IS BUZZING. I can't think, I can barely speak. It takes all my concentration to drive to my place knowing that Harper is right here beside me and she's coming home with me. We stumble out of the car and rush inside. Her cheeks are flushed from the cold winter air when we get to my door. I steal a kiss before opening the door for her.

We take the elevator to the top floor and stumble inside, lips already interlocked and bodies separated by many layers of thick winter clothing. Harper giggles as she takes off her hat and gloves and starts unbuttoning her long coat.

"This isn't quite so sexy when you have to spend ten minutes taking off all your layers," she laughs as she kicks off her boots.

"I still think it's sexy," I say, pulling her in for another kiss. I've never tasted lips that are so sweet. It feels like she melts into my arms whenever we touch. My whole body is tense with excitement.

I wrap my arms around her and pull her into me. My cock is throbbing, aching for her already. She shivers slightly in my arms and I pull her in closer, letting my fingers slide to the nape of her neck as she wraps her arms around me. It feels too good to be close to her, it shouldn't be allowed.

"Come on," I say in a hoarse whisper. I take her hand and guide her to my bedroom. She climbs onto the bed and in an instant I'm there with her, my body sinking down onto hers. I try to prop myself up on my arms to stop my body from crushing hers. Harper doesn't let me. She wraps her legs around me and pulls me down until our bodies sink into the bed and I can feel the warmth of her desire pressing against my stomach. She shivers again and moans before kissing me. I can feel her body vibrating under mine. It feels like a coiled spring, ready to explode as soon as I find the switch to release it.

Everything I've been dreaming of for the past three weeks is happening. Every look, every moment I've had at the office where all I could think about was her is coming to a head. I feel like my body is floating and flying through space at the same time. I can see every detail of her skin, every strand of hair, every freckle, every perfect curve and at the same time I can hardly focus on anything except the heat of her body and the hardness of my cock.

I'm panting as my lips find her ear, her neck, her clavicle. My kisses cover her soft white skin and I feel her hands fist into my hair. It's electric, the way she touches me. I slip my hand under her shirt and feel the softness of the skin on her stomach.

I run my fingers up her stomach and cup her breast, loving the way she moans as I feel her grind her hips into me. She feels better, she tastes better, she smells better than I remembered. She sits up and I help her slip off her shirt. The breath almost leaves my body. She has a freckle right below her left breast and I dip down to kiss it. My lips devour her skin. I can't stop kissing and tasting every inch of her. I'm addicted.

She's letting out tiny moans as my mouth moves down her stomach towards the hem of her pants. I can feel the heat between her legs even through the fabric. She runs her fingers through my hair and grinds her hips up towards me. I lift my chin and our eyes meet. I can't help but grin.

"Don't stop kissing me," she breathes as I run my hands over her thighs. My fingers dip under the hem of her pants and I run them across her stomach, feeling just a fraction of an inch closer to her centre.

Harper shivers and I lower my head down, kissing her pants in that crease between her leg and her hip. Her legs fall open and I can tell she wants me just as much as I want her.

I thought I'd have her completely naked by now. I thought we'd be at each other like animals. I thought the second she was in my bed my cock would be buried inside her and I could feel her pussy gripping down on me, but all I want to do right now is watch this beautiful woman shiver and moan as I touch her. I want to make her feel the way she makes me feel. I want to take my time and savour every second we have together.

Never has a woman had this effect on me. Watching her body react to my touch, to my lips, to my voice—it makes me almost insane with desire. It feels like our bodies know each other and everything happens by instinct. Her hand runs over my shoulder just as I reach up to trail my hands up her side. Her fingers tangle into my hair just as I dip my head down to kiss her stomach. Her hips tilt upwards just as I reach down to unfasten her pants. She moves, I move. It's the most erotic dance I've ever seen.

I hook my fingers into her pants and slide them down her thighs. Tossing them aside, my hands fly back to her legs and I run my fingers all the way back up to her panties.

I can't help it, I dip my head down and kiss the fabric, right where her clit is underneath it. I feel Harper exhale as she leans into the sensation. I breathe in deeply and I can just smell the sweet saltiness of her desire. My cock throbs and I dip down to kiss her again. She wraps her hands into my hair and tilts her hips up so that my lips meet the thin fabric of her panties again. I grip the sides of her hips and sink my fingers into her flesh. I find that crease between her leg and her hip and I let my tongue trail along the edge of her panties.

Harper lets out a soft moan and my cock pulses again. I can feel the heat between her legs and I can't take it anymore. I rip her panties off in one smooth movement. Harper's legs fall open and I exhale when I see her slit. It's pink and glistening and I'm aching to sink my length into her.

I won't let myself. I can't let myself, not now. Not with her like this, lying in my bed with her legs spread. My body is screaming for me to sheathe myself inside but first I have to taste her. I dive down and grip her hips, squeezing her between my fingers. The instant my mouth makes contact with her slit I hear her let out a laboured breath and her back arches.

Her wetness hits my tongue and I see stars. I've never tasted anything like this before. I'm not licking her, I'm devouring her. She's moaning and I'm moaning and my mouth is claiming her hungrily as her back arches and her fingers sink into my shoulders. Her nails dig into my flesh and the pain only serves to heighten the pleasure coursing through my veins.

I find her clit and swirl my tongue around it, feeling the hard bud between my lips as her moans get more pitched. There's a fever between us, a tension, a passion. I can't stop until I make this woman shudder and moan while my mouth ravages her.

I'm claiming her. She's mine.

23

HARPER

IN THIS MOMENT I'm totally and completely his. I'm under his spell. I'm lost. My body is trembling and I feel like I'm on the edge of consciousness. It doesn't matter. Nothing matters except the feeling of his lips between my legs and his tongue swirling as my orgasm builds.

I've never had a man touch me like this, taste me like this. He's doing more than tasting me, he's claiming my body in its entirety. My legs are shaking as he wraps his arms around my thighs, pushing my legs over his shoulders. His fingers slide down below his mouth and twirl around my opening, teasing me.

My body aches for him. The emptiness inside me is almost unbearable. His fingers torment me, sliding through my honey slick desire as they tease my opening and I feel my body contract around the nothingness. I need something. I need to be filled. I need *him*.

As if he senses my ache, he plunges his fingers inside me and takes my clit between his lips at the same time. The heat explodes between my legs and I force myself to look down at him. His eyes are closed and he moans as he tastes me again. I can feel his passion and it sends me even deeper into the ocean of pleasure that's washing over me.

He's enjoying this almost as much as I am.

Zach drags his fingers out of me and then plunges back in and I know that's a lie. There's no way he could be enjoying this as much as me. Every time he moves it sends a new wave of fire coursing through my veins.

He takes me closer and closer until finally the pressure inside me becomes too much. The heat building up between my legs erupts and I'm screaming, moaning, wailing wordlessly as his fingers and his mouth deliver the ultimate pleasure. My body lets go and I feel a flood of bliss crashing over me like a tidal wave.

It's not like my other orgasms. Instead of quenching my desire it only heightens it. As soon as the wave of pleasure subsides my eyes fly open and I sit up, pushing Zach off me and turning him over onto his back. He grins and complies without resistance.

"I was enjoying that," he reproaches.

"Why do you get all the fun?" I reply with a smile. Before he can respond, I'm taking his pants and underwear off and wrapping my fingers around his thick cock. It's hard and hot in my hand and it makes my body ache even more. I want him. I want him more than anything I've ever wanted before.

I know what it feels to have that cock inside me. It's indescribable, and it's going to be inside me again. I exhale as I stroke it, slowly at first and then faster. I glance up at him and I see his eyes half-closed in a daze. He's watching me, his eyes roaming over my breasts, my stomach, the glistening slit between my legs, and finally my hand wrapped around his shaft.

"That feels so good," he rasps.

I have to taste it. I lower my lips and take his cock hungrily into my mouth. Right now, I'm not trying to be sexy. I'm not trying to tease him or wow him with my sensual prowess. Right now, I just want his cock deep in my mouth. I want to feel it hit the back of my throat and I want my eyes to water as he drives it deeper into me. I want to feel his body tense and his cock pulse between my lips. I want to hear his grunts and moans turn primal as his cock enters my mouth over and over and over again.

I want it all.

I close my eyes and let my mouth move up and down his shaft. His moans mix with mine as I take him in my mouth from the tip to the hilt. He moves his hip and drives his cock down my throat, just barely making me choke. I love the way it feels to have him between my lips. I can feel my own wetness dripping out of me as his cock pulses and thrusts in and out of my mouth. He curls his fingers into my hair and pushes my head down onto his cock.

Zach pulls my hair slightly and gasps. "Harper," he breathes. "Harper I'm going to come, stop."

I lift my head slightly and see his face, wide-eyed and open-mouthed staring back at me. His chest is heaving up and down. I grin and lower my head back down. I want him to feel how I just felt. I part my lips and take his cock slowly, inch by inch, into my waiting mouth. He groans and shudders when I start bobbing my head up and down faster and faster. His cock hits the back of my throat and I feel him get even harder.

When he comes it sends pleasure coursing through my entire body. I run my hands over his chest and stomach as he bucks and convulses, his cock still buried deep down my throat. Zach's hand squeezes my hair until his body relaxes and I swallow the white seed that's filled my mouth.

My own body is vibrating with pleasure. I can feel my centre pulsing with desire. I'll have to wait to satisfy it, but I don't mind.

Finally, I lift my head and his cock slides out slowly. I crawl back up to lay beside him and he throws his arm across me, his eyes closed as he draws in one ragged breath after another.

"Jesus," he sighs as his eyes flutter open. I smile. I've never enjoyed giving a man an orgasm quite as much as I enjoyed that.

24

HARPER

THERE'S a thin film of sweat all over Zach's body, and I can feel my hair matted against my head. I don't care though, not even a little bit. Zach chuckles and shifts onto his side to face me. His pillows are soft and silky and his bed feels like it's made of clouds.

"I was dreading spending the holidays at the office, but it's turned out better than expected," he says, trailing his fingers up my arm and along my collarbone. I shiver at the sensation, my body still buzzing from the orgasm that just rocked through me and the adrenaline of making him come so hard.

"Between pulling down the tree and then sobbing into your shoulder it's a wonder you're interested in me at all," I laugh.

Zach laughs and I watch as his face brightens. His teeth are perfectly white and straight, and when he laughs his whole face transforms. I still can't believe I'm in my boss's bed. I feel a warmth pass through me and I smile with him.

"Is it too soon to laugh yet? God, Harper, you pulling down that tree was one of the funniest things I've ever seen."

He's laughing again and I can't help but chuckle. I playfully slap his arm.

"Stop," I say.

"You just had to get the biggest tree, didn't you? Exponential growth of Christmas cheer with every extra foot of height, if I remember correctly?"

"Well, I wasn't wrong," I protest.

"You want to show me that graph again, I think you missed the part about the tree smashing to the ground."

Before I can say any more his lips are crushed against mine and his fingers are tangling into my hair. He smells like musk and the weight of his body presses me down into the plush bed. I feel like I'm dreaming, or floating, or both.

His body is smooth and hard and I can feel his muscles rippling under his skin. He moves his hand down the side of my body, squeezing my waist and then reaching up to cup my breast. I shiver under his touch.

I don't know what it is about him but every time he touches me it's like it sets my body on fire. His hands are strong and warm, and the way he touches me sends sparks flying off my skin. I wrap my arms around him and curl my fingers into his back, feeling the hardness of his muscles under my touch.

Zach shifts his weight and sits up on his elbows, framing my face with his arms. His body feels heavy over mine, but in a comfortable way. He strokes the side of my face with a finger and then grins.

"Just one more question," he says, his eyes betraying a mischievous gleam. "About the tree. I've been wondering this ever since it happened."

I pretend to roll my eyes and then laugh. "What?"

"What were you doing to it? From where I was it looked

like you almost pulled it down on top of you on purpose." He grins and I feel my cheeks get red as the warmth of my embarrassment spreads all the way down my neck. I'll never live this down.

"I was just adjusting the decorations," I explain.

"The decorations were perfect, you know they were."

I sigh, and then laugh. I close my eyes and take a breath, trying not to let myself relive the event. "Truthfully I'd just been trying to avoid this guy. Rosie and I had gone over to the tree to pretend like we had something to do." I open my eyes and look at him. "I know, I know it's silly! But you don't understand Zach, sometimes it can be almost impossible to get away from him. Desperate times, you know?"

I'm expecting him to laugh or tease me but his face darkens.

"Who were you avoiding?"

My heart starts to beat harder as I see the seriousness of his question. Something in the air has shifted from playfulness to concern. I don't know how to answer. I don't want to tell him about my troubles last year, or the amount of fear and paranoia that I was living with.

All I want to do is enjoy this moment, and enjoy our time together. I want to feel this intimacy with him and have a lazy morning tomorrow. I want to have sex again and again and again until I have to go back to my regular job and Zachary Lockwood will go back to being my elusive boss.

"Harper, answer me." His voice is hard. "Who were you avoiding?"

"Greg Chesney. He... I..." my voice trails off. I don't know what to tell him. "I had to lodge a complaint against him but HR took over. It's just awkward now, it's not a big deal."

I feel Zach's body tense on top of me. His eyes are burning brighter than I've ever seen them.

"Greg Chesney from accounts?"

I've never seen him speak like this. His voice is hard and low, almost a growl.

"Yes," I reply slowly. "Do you know him?" My heart is still pounding in my chest and I wonder what Zach knows.

"I do now." He glances at me and I can see something shift in his eyes. There's an edge to them that I've never seen before and it almost scares me. Suddenly he jumps ups and goes to his closet. He's rummaging around for a few minutes and I prop myself up onto my elbows to watch.

After a few moments he reappears. He's completely naked, holding something out in front of him. I frown and sit up completely.

"Is that my ring?!" He hands it to me and my heart starts thumping. "How did you get this?!"

Zach says nothing, just sits on the edge of the bed and puts his head in his hands. He sits up and turns to me. I look from him to my ring and back to him again before slipping it onto my finger.

"Zach, answer me," I say again. "How did you get this?"

25

ZACH

My voice catches in my throat as Harper stares at me. It's her ring. The warning was to stay away from *her*! There's a deep uneasiness inside me. I can still see the way Greg looked at me with such hatred before his face went blank at the Christmas party. He looked like a psychopath.

"I got the ring delivered to me in a box with a note." I uncrumple the note from my hand and hold it out towards her. "What happened, Harper? How do you know Greg?"

"Greg sent this?? How did he get my ring? He must have gone into my office, looked through my stuff..." I can almost feel Harper's panic rising as the seconds tick by. Maybe I shouldn't have shown her the note.

"I don't know who sent it. All I know is it was sent to me yesterday."

"And he's disappeared...". She shakes her head. "No. I'm not going to let fear rule me. I've spent too many months looking over the shoulder. It's in the past now. HR were very clear that they did everything they could, and then I got promoted and I don't have to see him anymore. They said I had no evidence. And what kind of evidence is this?" She holds up the paper. "It doesn't have his name on it. It could be from anyone. Anyone could have seen me."

"Harper, who else would send it?" I ask gently. I put a hand on her leg and she looks at me, her eyes pleading with me.

"What am I supposed to do?"

I nod and lay down beside her, pulling her into my arms. I roll onto my back and stare at the ceiling as she rests her head on my chest.

It was her. He was stalking *her*. Harper, of all people! *MY* Harper!! A wave of rage starts building inside me. I can feel the heat of my anger gathering in my stomach, constricting my throat as I think about his weasel face. I didn't even know he existed until a couple days ago! How can I not know what's going on in my own company!

"I'm going to get to the bottom of this. That little fucker didn't even show up to work this week and no one knows where he is. I'm going to find proof and fire him, and then I'm going to the police."

"Zach, no!" Harper exclaims. Surprised, I turn to face her. Her face is drawn with worry. "If it ever came back on me, if he ever found out that I was the one to lose him his job..." she trails off, staring at me. I can see the fear clouding her green eyes.

She closes her eyes for a second. "I'm scared," she whispers. "He knows where I live."

A surge of emotion rushes through me. Harper looks so small, so powerless, so *scared*. I don't remember the last time I saw real fear in someone's eyes, and seeing it in hers makes my stomach curdle. I simultaneously want to jump up and smash a window and wrap my arms around her and never let go.

Harper makes a noise and I look down to see a tear rolling down her cheek. A dagger passes through my chest and then my arms are around her and I'm pulling her into me. I'm cooing and shushing into her ear, saying whatever comes out of my mouth to make her feel safe.

"Don't worry," I say. "I'm here, you're safe. Don't worry." I don't know how this has happened, how it is that I have Harper in my bed, in my arms right now but I don't want to let her go.

She pulls away slightly. "Promise me you won't do anything rash. You can look into him, but please don't fire him. Not right away. Not until I figure out the best move. He's not stable. If we set him off..." She doesn't finish her sentence but the words hang between us.

I want to say no. I want to tell her she's being ridiculous, that if this guy was stalking her to the point that a year later she still feels uncomfortable around him then I *can* and I *will* fire him on the spot and do everything in my power to get him arrested. But she's looking at me and her eyes are begging me, pleading with me to listen to her.

I nod, and then place a soft kiss on those intoxicating lips of hers. I can't pretend to understand, but I can tell she's serious. She's shaking, and I pull her in closer to me.

This is strange, this feeling. I can feel her fear as if it was my own and all I want to do is make it go away. All I want to do is put a smile on her face and see her eyes light up. Every time a cloud passes over her I feel it in my chest as if it were a red hot blade searing through my flesh. I can't explain it, I don't understand it, but somehow I care more about Harper than I've cared about any woman before.

Harper leans her head against my shoulder and trails her fingertips ever so gently along my collarbone. I close my eyes and lay into her, wrapping my arms around her a little bit tighter. Right now, I know that I'll do anything in the world for this woman.

I've had plenty of women in this bed, but I've never wanted one of them to stay. But here, with Harper, I don't think I've ever been this comfortable. There's something different about her. She can laugh and banter, and then she can turn into the most sensual, erotic woman I've ever encountered.

I'll get to the bottom of this Greg Chesney thing. I won't be able to let it go until I know what happened and I know Harper is safe. Before the anger has time to flare up, Harper starts grinding her body ever so gently against mine.

More important than anything else right now though is the beautiful woman in my bed with her arms wrapped around my body. My cock is done thinking about anything except Harper Anderson and the way her naked body feels when it's pressed against mine.

26

HARPER

Z ACH IS different from what I expected. I've heard all the stories: womaniser, playboy, commitment-phobe. Every time I've seen him he always has a new woman on his arm. I thought sex at the office would bit it, but here I am waking up next to him in his huge king-sized bed. Even last night, there was no question about me going back to my apartment. We fell asleep with our bodies intertwined as if they belonged together.

I watch him as he sleeps, his face completely peaceful, and I remember the look of anger that clouded his brow when we were talking about Greg Chesney. Was that anger on my behalf? How much does he know? Was he angry because he cares about me or because it's bad for the company?

He's been so... affectionate. I can't wrap my mind around it. It's so easy to be around him but at the same time he's my boss, and all evidence points to him being a total player. I thought I'd be sleeping alone tonight, replaying our first time in the office over and over in my head like every other night since it happened and instead I'm here, in his penthouse, replaying our first time, and our second time, and our third time...

He inhales sharply and snorts and I try not to laugh. I don't want to wake him. I slip out of the bed gently and find my clothes. I saw a cafe just on the corner when we drove up last night, and for the first time in over a week, coffee sounds amazing right now. The minute the thought crosses my mind I get an incredible craving for it. I'll get us both a coffee and a pastry and we can have breakfast in bed together, and then hopefully we can give me some more daydream material with our fourth and fifth times. Maybe sixth time, if I'm lucky.

I grab his keys and wrap myself in my jacket before taking the elevator down. He lives on the thirty-seventh floor, and the view of Manhattan is insane. It's even better than the view from the office. The whole wall of the elevator is made of glass, so I can see the ground rushing up towards me. It's a perfect bluebird day, with clear skies and bright sunlight. There's a fresh layer of white snow on every surface.

It's only a short walk to the cafe. The bell jingles as I walk in and the young man behind the counter greets me. He has a low ponytail and a moustache, and the carefully dishevelled look of a true hipster. The smell of coffee beans is almost overwhelming, and I feel a wave of nausea hit me. What is wrong with me?! Every morning I feel like I'm going to be sick. I take a deep breath and steady myself against a chair. In an instant my nausea turns to craving. I don't know what is wrong with my body these days.

"One Americano and one large latte with no sugar, please," I tell the barista. I'm pretty sure I've heard him order a latte before, but I can't be certain. Either way it's what he's getting. I pick out a couple pastries and pay.

When the coffee is ready I grab them with the paper bag of warm baked goods and try to balance them in my hands as I push the door open. The bell jingles and I see something, or *someone* out of the corner of my eye. The man jumps up from a bench and turns towards me. I try to look but the bright sunlight reflecting against the snow blinds me for a second. My eyes adjust a second too late.

A man walks right by me and I swear I know him. He jumps into a car and drives off. I spin around and stare into the car as it passes me, but he had his head turned and the brightness is still piercing my eyes. I squint, trying to read the license plate number but it's too late. He's gone.

I didn't know that car, but a cold chill passes down my spine. I could have sworn I recognised that slouchy walk, that height, that build. He was wearing baggy clothes and a hat, looking away from me so I never got a look at his face. My heart is thumping in my chest as my eyes finally adjust to the light.

I stare down the street, looking up and down as the people mill past me. The world tilts on its axis and I struggle to stay standing. I feel like I've just sprinted down the street but I've been standing still, the hot coffee slowly warming up my hands.

Surely it wasn't him, right? What would Greg Chesney be doing here?

The earth slowly shifts back to it's normal position and I glance up and down the street. Everything looks normal. I'm just freaked out. I've been looking over my shoulder for a year, and we were talking about him last night, that's all. With the ring, and the note, I'm just on edge.

It wasn't him. It couldn't be him!

I take a deep breath and turn towards the building. It wasn't him. Now that I think about it, it looked like this guy had curly hair under his hat, and Greg's hair is very straight. It was just some other New Yorker who was in a rush to get somewhere. I'm just extra jumpy from yesterday. It wasn't him. It wasn't him. It definitely wasn't him.

I say these things to myself over and over, all the way back up the elevator and into the apartment. By the time I open the door and put the drinks down to take my jacket off, my heart rate has gone back to normal and the prickly feeling at the back of my neck is almost gone. I'm back here, with Zach. I'm safe.

Taking a deep breath, I grab the coffees and food and head into the bedroom. I need to forget about Greg Chesney and focus on where I am. I don't know how long this is going to last, so I might as well enjoy every second of it. I'm with the man I've been fantasising about for the past two years, and he's sexier than I could have imagined, and he wants *me.*

My stalker is in the past. The fear and paranoia is in the past. Greg has been disciplined and dealt with. It's over.

It's time I enjoyed myself, for once! I deserve some good sex and a little bit of office romance. I push the bedroom door open and walk in just as Zach opens his eyes. He smiles sleepily.

"That smells good," he breathes.

"Large latte, no sugar?" I ask. He opens his eyes and nods, sitting up in bed.

"You are unbelievably good, Harper. Did you know that?"

"I have many talents," I say with a cheeky smile.

"I'm discovering that," he replies as he takes his coffee. Instead of taking a sip, he puts his hand around the nape of my neck and pulls me in for a deep kiss. I lean into him and kiss him back, loving every single second we have together. I pull away and smile.

"First, coffee and croissants. Then we do that."

He grins. "You drive a hard bargain, Harper. Deal."

27

ZACH

It's uncharted territory for me, wanting a woman to stay with me. I can't explain it, and I don't understand it, but it's true. I want her here. I want her beside me, around me, on top of me. I want her sex and her voice and her laugh and her eyes. I want to experience everything about her and learn all there is to learn about her. I want to make her laugh and make her orgasm and then make her laugh again.

The next week turns into a haze of work, overtime, takeout eaten at the office, sex, early mornings with Harper, and more work. I get a small turkey dinner catered in for Christmas, but otherwise it could be any other week. In the evenings, Harper comes back to my place for wild nights and happy mornings. I love having her in my bed every night and waking up next to her in the morning. I love the way she looks sleepy when she wakes up, and how her auburn hair looks dark against my white pillows.

I watch her working at the office and I'm constantly amazed at her skills at work. She executes the plan perfectly, pushing the team to produce some of the best content we've produced as a company. I don't even really need to be here.

I'm sitting in my office and I watch her leaning over Rosie's desk, looking at one of our advertising proposals. She tucks a strand of hair behind her ear and points to something on the desk. I can't hear what they're saying, but she starts gesturing, explaining what she wants. Rosie is listening intently and then nods. Harper smiles and says something and then they both laugh. I can't help but smile along. Harper glances up and catches me staring at her. She smiles and winks before walking towards her own office.

I love the way Harper laughs with her mouth wide open. It's loud and unapologetic. She throws her head back and her laugh ripples through her whole body, making it impossible not to laugh along. No wonder everyone likes her—the minute she flashes that smile or laughs at one of your jokes, all you want to do is make it happen again. It's all I want to do, anyways.

Glancing at my calendar, I shake my head and sigh. This is not the New Year's Eve I'd imagined. It hasn't been bad, quite the opposite. In many ways this holiday season has been the best I've had in years. I just never imagined I'd be sitting behind my desk at 4pm on December 31st, working on a proposal that was supposed to be due at the end of next month.

My computer dings and I look at my inbox.

FROM: *Harper Anderson*
Subject: *Latif Proposal*

I click the email and smile. She's done it, and an entire day early as well. I open the file and am looking it over when there's a knock on the doorframe. Harper is leaning against it with a playful smile in her eyes.

"Just sent that through to you," she says.

"I'm looking at it now. I like the changes you've made to the first ad set," I say as I glance back at the screen. I read through the document and look up again. Harper is still in the doorway. "This is very good."

"We have a good team," she responds, always modest about her work.

"We have a good leader," I tell her. She smiles shyly. I turn back to my computer and pull up the email I've already drafted. I attach the file and take a deep breath. I glance up at Harper and grin. "Do you want to do the honours?"

Her smile widens and she practically jumps forward. "Yes!"

She comes around my desk and I present my mouse to her. With great ceremony and flourish, she places her delicate hand over the mouse and hovers over the 'Send' button. Before pressing it she glances at me and gently pushes her shoulder into mine.

"This is it," she says with a grin.

"Do it!"

She clicks the mouse and my computer makes the familiar 'whoosh' sound as the email is sent. It's done. Harper stands up and puts her hands on her hips. My hand drifts up and grazes the curve of her ass. She makes a soft noise before turning back towards me.

"Should we go tell the team?"

"Yes, and then we can celebrate."

"Definitely."

Her green eyes are shimmering and I can tell she's happy. She should be! She's just saved the firm a major client just in time to ring in the New Year. The two of us walk around my desk and I try not to stare at the way her hips move from side to side. I'll have those hips between my hands as soon as I can. I'll pull her into me and lay her down before spreading her perfect legs. My mouth waters at the thought of tasting her.

I pull myself away from my daydream as we walk out into the main room. I hold up my hands.

"Team, thank you for your incredible effort over the past week. I'm happy to say the Latif proposal has just been sent. I know many of you have families and friends to go back to, and you're free to go.

The half dozen employees cheer and clap. Harper is beaming.

"If any of you are like me, with no friends to speak of," laughter ripples through the team. "Then please join me downstairs for a few drinks, on me. Happy New Year!"

"Happy New Year!" Comes the answer, echoing through our small holiday team. Harper goes over to Rosie and the two of them hug each other. Rosie says something I can't quite catch and Harper laughs before waving her hand dismissively. The two of them glance at me and Harper blushes.

I can't help but grin. I love the way her white skin flushes so easily. I can't wait to make her blush even more tonight.

28

HARPER

THIS IS the hardest I've ever worked, but it doesn't feel like it. I've never put so many hours in to finish a project but the only real memory I have from this week is my time in Zach's arms. His voice is deep and triumphant as he announces to our small team that the proposal has been sent. I watch the way his shirt pulls against his shoulders as he raises his arms towards the employees. He turns to me and smiles and I feel my knees go weak. That smile knocks me out every time.

I turn to Rosie and congratulate her.

"Couldn't have gotten this over the line without you, Rosie," I say. She smiles and opens her arms up for a hug.

"Stop, Harper. You know you carried us all this week."

She lets go of me and I take a step back. She cocks her head to the side and I see a mischievous gleam in her eye.

"Plus," she adds. "I'm impressed you've been able to do it considering you haven't been getting any sleep at night."

I can't help it, I start laughing. I can feel the flush in my cheeks creeping from my face out to my ears. I don't say anything, because she's right. I haven't been sleeping much but I feel more energised than ever. Every time Zach touches me or looks at me it's like a bolt of lightening right through me.

We all gather our things and head down into the cold New York winter. We make it to the same bar we go to for all our team events and stumble in the door. It's already half-full of people in sparkly hats, drinking as the New Year approaches.

Zach makes his way to the bar and speaks to the bartender, who produces half a dozen bottles of champagne. It's almost one bottle each and I start laughing.

"Don't you think this is a bit much? There's only eight of us!"

"We have a lot to celebrate!" Zach says. He turns to me and it almost looks like he'll lean down and kiss me before he catches himself. He hands me a champagne flute and pours them for everyone else. We all raise our glasses. Zach clears his throat.

"To a successful proposal, and a healthy and happy New Year!"

"Happy New Year!" We respond, echoing him before clinking our glasses together in a circle and taking a sip. I look around the team and I can't help but feel a burning in my heart. I'm proud of our work, proud of our team, proud of myself. For the first time I feel like I get to share that pride and happiness with someone else.

The bubbles explode on my tongue and I feel a small shiver travel down my spine. I love champagne. I glance up at Zach and find him looking at me. His eyes are deep and I see something like a current of happiness in them. He lets his hand drift to the small of my back and I lean into him ever so slightly. From where we're standing at the bar, no one can see the movement and it feels like our little secret. Even just standing next to him feels more intimate than I could imagine.

He fills up my glass and the bubbles rush and climb up the sides, trying to escape out the top. Right before the bubble over, the liquid turns golden and settles down. I giggle. Everything about champagne is excited and happy, and it's exactly how I feel right now. Zach's hand presses into my back and drifts down. His fingertips brush the cleft of my ass and I shiver. The wetness between my legs soaks through my panties in an instant as his fingers ever so gently travel down the line of my ass.

I take a sip of champagne to hide my constantly blushing cheeks. With my nose buried in the glass, I close my eyes and lean into him a tiny bit more. His hand cups my ass and gives it a soft squeeze. The warmth of his hand as he squeezes sends a jolt of desire coursing through my veins. I don't think I'll make it to midnight. All I want to do is ring in the New Year with his cock buried deep inside me.

As if he can read my mind, he leans over and whispers in my ear. The heat of his breath tickles my neck and I try to focus on his words instead of the warmth radiating between my legs.

"Let's get out of here," he breathes. "You are driving me wild."

"So are you," I reply.

"I'll go first," he says. "I'll wait for you in the car. Don't be too long this time."

I grin. It's our usual routine. To avoid gossip, we never leave the office together. We typically stagger our exit by ten or fifteen excruciating minutes. As soon as he makes his goodbyes I know I won't last that long. Five, six minutes tops.

The seconds drag on one by one as I wait for my opportunity to leave.

Rosie slides in beside me. "So I guess you'll be leaving in what, seven or eight minutes? Do you guys have a timer set?"

I glance at her sideways and start to laugh. "Is it that obvious?"

"Only to me," she grins. "I don't think anyone else knows."

"Good."

"They've only just gotten over the tree incident, I think an affair with New York's sexiest boss would be too much. You'd never recover," she says with an exaggerated sigh.

"I can't believe this is all happening."

"You deserve it, Harper. You've worked your ass off and been through so much. Why not you! Why not be happy!"

Rosie turns to me and puts her glass of champagne down on the bar. She puts her hands on my shoulders and gives them a squeeze. Her eyes are shining and it looks like she's about to cry. My throat tightens as I wait for her to speak.

"You're the best friend I could ask for, Harper. When all that stuff with Greg was happening last year it scared me and broke my heart. The way you and Zach look at each other just makes me so happy for you. Don't be afraid of this. You are amazing, and you deserve an amazing man by your side."

My eyes start prickling as the tears gather in the corner. My throat feels like it's almost completely closed and I try to swallow before answering.

"Rosie, that's such a nice thing to say." She smiles and blinks a few times, trying to hold back her emotion.

"I mean it. Now go," she laughs. "If you're able to walk tomorrow I'll be very disappointed. You have some celebratory sex to have!"

I laugh and wrap my arms around her. She's right, we

have lots to celebrate so we might as well get started as soon as possible. There's a bounce in my step as I walk out of the bar. I check the time before laughing to myself. I barely lasted four minutes in there on my own. My body wants what it wants, who am I to deny myself that kind of pleasure?!

Zach is in his car. The passenger's side door swings open as I get close and a wave of heat falls out of the car. I climb in and close the door before turning to him and crushing my lips against his. The taste of champagne is still on my lips but his kiss tastes a million times better.

"Let's get out of here," he says when we pull apart. His eyes are shining in the dim light and all I can do is nod. That's exactly what I want to do.

29

ZACH

HARPER'S BODY feels like a dream. She feels small and perfect underneath me, both our bodies sinking into the bed together. Her skin is incredibly soft, and my hands run all over her from top to bottom. My lips kiss her ear, her neck, her shoulder. I trail my kisses down between her breasts before taking one of her nipples between my lips. I open my teeth and bite gently as she whimpers and moans. Her fingers are tangled into my hair and I feel her squeeze a little bit tighter. It sends tiny thrills of pain and pleasure through my skull.

Her stomach is white and soft. Every inch of her skin has a sweet smell that invades my nostrils and makes my cock impossibly hard. I move down and run my hands from her feet up her legs, closer and closer to the glistening slit between them. I resist the urge to plunge my cock straight into her, as much as my body is screaming for it.

Our bodies know each other and she moves as if she knows what I'm going to do a second before I do it. It's intimate, it's magic. Her hands are on my back, my arms, my chest. She wraps her fingers around my cock and I have to closer my eyes for a second to regain control over my own body. I drag my fingers through her wetness and bring them up to her mouth just as she parts her lips to accept them.

"Taste yourself," I breathe. My voice is hoarse and I watch in amazement as her lips take my fingers. Her tongue swirls around them and she moans as the flavour of her pussy touches it. My cock pulses as I watch her. I'm jealous of her tongue, I wish that taste was on mine. I slide my fingers out and see Harper's eyes burning with carnal desire. Slowly, deliberately, I taste what's left of her on my fingers. I close my eyes and savour the sweet saltiness as it hits my tongue.

I want more.

Harper's legs squeeze me as she wraps them around my waist. I can feel the heat pulsing from between her legs and my cock is pressed against her hipbone. She wraps herself around me and pulls me in closer, crushing her lips against mine. She lets out a soft moan. I catch the sound between her lips and take it into my own. My hands find the back of her head and I wrap her hair around my fingers to pull her in closer.

I can't let her go. I don't want to let her go. I want every inch of me inside every inch of her. As if she reads my mind, she shifts her hips and my cock slides down between her legs. Even with just the tip of it grazing her slit, I feel the wetness of her desire.

When I finally enter her it's like the first time. No, it's better than the first time. This is the pure Harper. She and I are completely free and flying as our bodies pant and grab and groan together. Her smell is intoxicating, her touch is electrifying. I plunge myself into her and she arches her back in response. Every sound she makes vibrates through me and sends new waves of pleasure coursing through my veins.

We turn and thrash. She's on top, I'm on top, our lips are interlocked, I'm taking her breast in my mouth. My hands grab at anything and everything—a hip, a leg, a hand, a breast. It's frantic. We tear at each other like animals. It's more raw, more real than anything I've experienced before.

Harper gasps as my cock plunges into her again before I take it out. It feels naked and all I want to do is dive back into her, but I grab her hips and turn her around. She tilts her ass towards me and glances over her shoulder with a devilish grin. I push my cock into her and gasp as she accepts it. My fingers run down her spine until I can grab a handful of that honey brown hair, pulling it back as she yelps and gasps. Her back is arched and she grabs onto my headboard before slamming her ass back into me.

"Harder," she says in a raspy voice. "Fuck me harder."

I've never heard her sound like this. It sends a current through me and I raise my hand to bring it down on her ass. The sharp crack of skin on skin sends a thrill through me and Harper makes the sexiest noise I've ever heard, halfway between a yelp and a moan.

"Again," she pants, and I comply. I leave a bright red handprint on her ass and then I smack it again. The only sound in the room is our two bodies colliding together and the sound of my hand spanking her over and over.

I feel her come. Her pussy spasms and floods with wetness. It grips my cock like never before and she starts moaning, grunting, screaming. She's screaming my name and I tighten my hold on her hair, slamming my cock into her again and again.

Finally my balls tighten up towards me and I feel the

sweet release of orgasm. I've been holding on, resisting, trying to make this moment last but I can't wait any longer. The electricity passes through me like a shock and I let go. I come, shaking and screaming as Harper backs herself onto my cock. I tighten my grip on her hair until my orgasm reaches its peak and then all energy leaves my body. I lean forward and the two of us collapse down until my lips connect with her back. I pant against her and kiss her skin, trying to regain control over my limbs.

I roll over onto my back as my chest heaves up and down. My arm falls over against her and she slips her hand into me. We say nothing to each other. We don't need to. I don't know what's just happened but I know it feels different. It was more intense than anything I've ever experienced before. It wasn't just sex, it wasn't just fucking. It was something more.

Turning my head, I open my eyes and see Harper collapsed on the pillow. Her hair is a mess where I was grabbing it and I can still see the red marks on her ass from my hand.

"You're a mess," I say with a grin.

Her green eyes sparkle as she looks at me. "So are you," she replies.

"I don't care."

"Neither do I."

Her replies are quick but her voice is soft and seductive. She doesn't take her eyes off me and it seems like she's looking through me, like she can see something inside me. I'm more exposed than I've ever been in my life. It's not bad though, it's the opposite—it feels better to be here like this, with her... better than I could have ever imagined.

30

HARPER

I FALL asleep feeling like I'm living a dream, but reality comes crashing down when I wake up and rush to the toilet. The nausea is overwhelming, and all I can do is stumble out of bed and sprint to the bathroom. I just barely make it in time, emptying the contents of my stomach into the white porcelain.

My stomach heaves and the bile burns my throat as I retch. My eyes water and I wait for the feeling to pass before flushing the toilet. I'm so consumed with nausea that I barely hear Zach get out of bed and follow me.

When the episode has passed, Zach's hand comes down onto my shoulder. The warmth of his large hand is comforting, and I wipe away the tears that escape my eyes.

"You okay?" He asks. His voice is deep and filled with worry.

"Yeah, I'm fine. I've been feeling a bit nauseous for the past couple weeks."

"Weeks?! Have you been to the doctor?"

I turn to see Zach squatting beside me, lines of worry

drawn on his forehead. He reaches over and strokes the side of my cheek. I close my eyes and lean into his hand.

"No, not yet. I was waiting to see if I'd get better."

"It might be some sort of stomach bug, two weeks is not normal. I'll take you to my doctor, he's really good."

"That's okay, Zach, really. All I need is some rest. We've been working like crazy I'm sure that's not helping."

Zach shakes his head. He runs his fingers over my temple and into my hair. His other hand grabs my hand and he helps me stand. After I rinse out my stale mouth, he brings me over to the bed. I lay down and close my eyes, focusing on the softness of the bed and the warmth of the blankets instead of the roiling in my stomach.

In a couple minutes a cup of tea materialises beside me with a few crackers.

"Eat something, and then I'm taking you to the doctor."

"Zach, really, I'm fine! I don't need a doctor."

He shakes his head and crosses his arms and I know I'm not going to win this one. I can't help it. Ever since my many appointments and tests, poking and prodding leading to the news that I was infertile, I've developed a strong dislike for doctors. Even the smell of the offices, the sterile plastic beds and crunch of the white paper, it all makes an uncomfortable feeling crawl down my spine.

Still, looking at Zach as he sits on the bed and hands me the cup of tea, I know he won't change his mind. I see real concern in his eyes and as much as I hate doctors, I can't help but feel comforted by the fact that Zach cares. He really cares! He *wants* to take care of me. It's not a chore at all.

He's putting my tea back on the side table and stroking my head as I lie back in bed. The nausea has passed and I feel a bit silly.

"I feel fine now," I start. Zach shakes his head.

"You're not getting away that easy," he grins. I can't help but smile back. "Why are you so against going to the doctor, anyways?"

I hesitate. I feel comfortable with him. I could tell him everything, about the months of tests and trying to have children only to find out I couldn't. The heartbreak of it all, and how it destroyed my relationship. I could tell him about the miscarriages and finally that doctor's cold, unfeeling word: infertile.

I could tell him, but I don't. I just shrug.

"Don't like doctors," I say as a weak explanation. Zach looks at me for a few moments but doesn't press me any further. He just gathers the dishes and stands up.

"Come on, babe, get dressed and I'll take you. Might be as simple as taking a round of antibiotics."

Babe.

My heart flutters at the word and Zach didn't even seem to notice. He turns around and brings the mug back to the kitchen as I lie in his bed with my heart thumping and my head spinning. I swing my legs off the bed and start putting my clothes on.

Looks like it's time to face my fears and go to the doctor. As much as it makes me nervous, there's also a warmth in my chest and a fluttering in my stomach when I think about Zach's eyes, his touch, his voice when he called me *babe*. He cares about me—truly cares about me.

I slip on my shirt and head out to the main room. Zach is bending over, putting some dishes in the dishwasher. I grin as I watch the way his ass pulls against the fabric of his pants. He stands up and looks over his shoulder.

"What are you laughing at?"

"You cute man bum," I reply. He turns around completely and leans on the counter, crossing his arms and raising an eyebrow.

"Man bum?"

"Yeah!" Both of his eyebrows are now shooting towards his hairline. I laugh. "Don't worry, yours is really nice. A+ man bum."

He grins and pushes himself off the counter, taking me in his arms.

"You're a big pervert, you know that Harper?"

Instead of replying, I slide my hands down his back and cup his ass. I give it a small squeeze and he laughs before tucking his chin down and placing a soft kiss on my lips. My heart cartwheels in my chest and I melt into his arms.

Suddenly the doctor doesn't seem so daunting.

31

ZACH

HARPER'S KNEE is bouncing up and down as we sit in the waiting room for her name to be called. I've never seen her like this. My Harper, usually so poised and collected, is a nervous wreck. She spins her head around and I see a hint of true fear in her eyes. Her soft pink lips part and she takes a deep breath.

"Will you come into the room with me? You know, for moral support?" She takes another breath and her eyes mist up. "I know it's pathetic, I'm sorry. You must think I'm ridiculous."

I put my hand on her knee and it slows to a stop. "You're not pathetic or ridiculous, Harper. Everyone needs a bit of help once in a while."

She nods. I watch as her eyes dart from the hallway to the doctor's offices, to the receptionist, to the other patients.

This is the woman who just led our team to deliver an extremely difficult and complex proposal under an incredible time crunch, and who did it without showing any hesitation. She's got the respect of her peers and employees, and yet she's afraid of a routine doctor's appointment? It doesn't add up. There must be something she's not telling me. She must have had a bad experience, maybe when she was a kid.

After what seems like an eternity, Doctor MacDonald appears in the hallway. I've been coming to see him for the past ten years, and I don't think he's changed at all. His shock of white hair is still a bird's nest on his head, and his wiry white eyebrows wiggle on top of his friendly blue eyes. If there was ever a doctor who gave off the Grandpa vibe, it's Doctor Mac. I can't think of a better man to take care of Harper, especially when she's so nervous.

"Harper? Harper Anderson?" Doctor Mac calls out as he scans the waiting room. Harper jumps up and starts walking before turning towards me. She holds out her hand and I stand up slowly, taking it in mine. Her hand is cold and clammy.

"I hope you don't mind if Zach comes in with me?" She asks. "I'm a bit nervous."

"Not at all," Doctor Mac says as he nods to me. "Good to see you again, Zachary."

His office is just like any other. There's an anatomy poster on the stark white walls, and jars of cotton balls and tongue depressors lined up on the counter. I sit down in a chair and Doctor Mac motions for Harper to sit on the blue plastic bed. The paper crunches as she sits down on top of it, and the doctor takes a seat at his computer. It's cramped with three of us in the small room.

"Now," he says in a smooth low voice, crossing his hands on his lap and turning towards her. "What seems to be the issue?"

Harper explains and the doctor keeps asking questions. Her hands are gripping the edge of the bed so hard her knuckles are turning white. I can see a vein in her neck pulsing as the blood pumps through. Her lips, usually full and pink with a beautiful soft curve, have turned into a thin line across her face.

All I want to do is sit next to her and put my arm around her. It kills me to see her like this. Finally Doctor Mac grabs a small jar from a drawer and takes it out of its sterile packaging.

"The bathroom is just down the hall to the left. If you can, fill it up to the line here," he points to a line three quarters of the way up. "Otherwise just get as much as you can."

Harper grabs the vial and nods.

"Good luck!" Doctor Mac says cheerily. I grin. He does have a gift for unwavering good humour. Harper glances at me before heading out the door. She closes it softly and I turn to Doctor Mac, who's typing notes on his computer.

"Do you think it's serious?"

"No way to tell," he replies. He types a few more words and then presses one last button with a flourish before turning towards me. "But she's walking and talking so I'd say she's in fairly good shape."

I chuckle. "I've never seen her so nervous!"

"Us doctors are a scary bunch!" He replies just as the door opens. Harper holds out the jar with her yellow urine in it. Looks like she was able to fill most of it up, and I silently tell her *good job.*

Doctor Mac snaps a blue latex glove onto his hand and grabs the jar. He slips it into a clear plastic bag and stands up.

"We can run a few tests right now, so if you don't mind waiting five or ten minutes, I'll be right back."

"Sounds good, thanks Doctor," Harper says, sitting back down on the examination table. Doctor Mac nods and slips out the door. I stand up and take a few steps until I'm standing in front of her. I put my hands on either side of her arms and give them a squeeze.

"It'll be okay. He's a great doctor."

"Yeah he's nice," she says with a weak smile. "Sorry, I've just had bad experiences at the doctor and now they make me nervous."

"I get it. I'm here for you." She nods, and I continue. "You hear me, Harper? I'm here for you. I'll take care of you, no matter what."

Her eyes lift up to mine and I feel a surge of emotion in my chest. Butterflies crash around my ribcage and stomach as I watch the sparkle in her green eyes.

"You mean it?" She whispers. "You'll take care of me?"

"Always." I take a deep breath. "I care about you, Harper. More than I've cared about anyone in a long, long time." *Ever, maybe.* "Plus, I've never had anyone tell me I have a cute man bum, and that's worth hanging onto."

She smiles and her eyes mist up. Her arms find my waist and she pulls me in closer. I hold her in my arms until her trembling body calms down. I stroke her head and place a soft kiss on her brown hair. Even when she's nervous and sick, she still smells like roses.

With Harper in my arms in the doctor's office, I know in my heart that I was telling the truth. I'll do anything for her.

32

HARPER

THE DOOR OPENS and Zach pulls away from me. I extract myself from the warmth of his arms and he goes back to his chair. We look at the doctor expectantly as he closes the door, holding a clipboard in his hand.

Doctor MacDonald turns to us and holds his arms out by his sides, palms facing us. He smiles.

"Congratulations!"

I frown, and glance at Zach. He looks from Doctor MacDonald to me and then back to the doctor.

Doctor MacDonald looks at me, beaming. "You're expecting!"

"Expecting what?" My brain can't process his words. I know what they mean, but I can't make any sense of it. Expecting?

"Expecting a child," he explains as his eyebrows twitch into a slight frown. "You're pregnant. Congratulations! What a perfect couple for it as well. Beautiful child, I'm sure." He sits down in front of his computer and starts typing something.

"We'll have to get you in for a checkup in the next couple weeks. Wonderful!"

The air rushes around my ears and I feel like I'm going to fall over. I turn towards the doctor and the paper under me crinkles and crunches.

"That's not possible," I say. My breath is short and my voice sounds strained, even to my ears. I don't have the nerve to look at Zach right now. I can hardly look at the doctor. I just keep repeating: "That's not possible."

Doctor MacDonald looks at me. I can't say anything else, so I just repeat myself one more time. "That's not possible." My throat is closing and the edges of my vision are going blotchy and dark.

"It is possible, and it's true," Doctor MacDonald says. "About three to four weeks, I'd say."

I do mental calculations. Three to four weeks... my jaw drops and I finally turn my head towards Zach. *The Christmas party!*

Zach's face is as white as a sheet. He's gripping the armrests and staring at Doctor MacDonald. He sees me turn towards him and lifts his eyes towards me. I can't read them, they're dark and cloudy. My voice is stuck in my throat and I don't know what to say. He stays silent.

"Oh my God," I breathe as I bring a hand up to my forehead. Should I be happy about this? This is all I wanted for years, but now... Is Zach happy? He doesn't look happy. He hasn't said anything.

Everything from the past few weeks rushes back towards me. The nausea, the cravings, the tiredness, the swollen fingers. I've been pregnant this whole time!

Doctor MacDonald is saying a thousand and one things and thrusting pamphlets into my hands. I take them but all I can hear is the gargled sound of his voice. It sounds like he's speaking to me under water, I can't make out anything he says. I try to focus, try to think. I'm sure it's important, but all I can think of is the last time I went to the doctor.

One in ten million.

Infertile.

Might as well be impossible.

Consider adoption.

Finally I look at Doctor MacDonald and interrupt him. "I'm infertile! This isn't possible."

He pauses, and tilts his head to the side. His eyes soften and he nods slowly. "It would appear the last doctor you went to made a mistake. Some people call them miracle babies."

"Miracle babies," I repeat. I glance at Zach, who's still as pale as a ghost and staring at the ground between his feet. He hasn't said a word. My heart starts thumping and I feel the panic welling up inside me.

Finally, the doctor says a few more unintelligible things and ushers us out the door. I walk out in a daze, making my way outside with Zach. He hasn't spoken and he won't look at me. I put a hand over my stomach and feel a flutter in my chest.

Miracle baby.

Suddenly the shock dissipates and I my heart starts beating with something new. I'm pregnant! I'm pregnant! I'm going to have a child!!

Zach unlocks his car and I slide into the passenger's seat. He puts the key in the ignition but doesn't start the car. I take a deep breath.

"Zach, listen, I..." I pause. "I was told before that it was impossible for me to have children. If you don't want to be a part of the kid's life, I understand. I'm willing to take care of it on my own. This wasn't something you planned for. Neither of us could have."

His head turns slowly around towards me. His eyes are blazing and he opens his mouth. I shy away from him, leaning back towards the car door. This isn't the caring man who was holding me in his arms just minutes ago.

"You..." he pauses and licks his lips. His eyes are dark and stormy and unreadable. "You're going to keep it?"

My stomach drops and my heart beats in my suddenly hollow chest. My eyes prickle and the anger flares up inside me. Am I going to keep it?! *Of course* I'm going to flipping keep it!

"Yes."

He stares at me for a few moments before nodding. He turns towards the steering wheel and turns the car on.

"I should probably take you home, then?"

His words pierce my chest like a hot dagger. He wants nothing to do with me. He just wants to get rid of me as soon as possible.

"Yeah," is the only response I can manage. I stare out the window as he starts driving, trying to choke back tears. Ten minutes ago he was telling me he would take care of me no matter what, and now he's dumping me off back home like I'm some sort of inconvenience. I get that this is unexpected, but does he have to be so *cold*?! He won't even look at me!

A tear rolls down my cheek and I brush it away quickly. It feels like a hand is squeezing my chest and I can hardly breathe. We drive in silence, staring out the window. The tortuous drive to my house finally ends as he pulls up in front of my apartment building.

"Thanks," I say. I turn towards him, wanting him to say something. I want him to say that it'll be okay, that we'll figure it out. I don't need him to marry me or stay with me or even be part of the baby's life but I do need to feel like he doesn't hate me all of a sudden.

"No problem," he says. He keeps staring straight ahead and doesn't look at me. The dagger in my chest twists and my vision goes blurry as the tears fill my eyes. I scratch at the door for the handle and stumble out of the car. As soon as I close the door, he's speeding off down the street.

I watch the car turn off and I break down. The tears come hot and fast, and my sobs shake through my entire body. I stumble into my building and crawl up the stairs. I'm crying so hard I can't see anything in front of me. My breath is ragged and I gulp in the air in between sobs. I struggle to unlock my door and finally push my way in, closing it behind me and collapsing onto the floor.

I cry and cry and cry, hugging my arms to my stomach. I'm alone now. Zach never cared about me at all. It was all just a fling, just a bit of fun to him. He was just telling me what I wanted to hear. The torrent of emotion inside me is like a hurricane.

When it quiets down all that's left are two words burned into my mind's eye: I'm alone. The tears are still streaming down my face but I force myself to stand up.

"It's just the two of us now," I whisper to my belly. "I'll take care of you."

I take a deep breath and head towards the bathroom. Bath, ice cream, and movies. Maybe Rosie will come over and she can help me figure out my life from there.

33

ZACH

I WALK into my apartment and I realise I don't remember the drive back to my place at all. I hardly remember leaving the doctor's office. I drop my keys on the counter and take off my jacket before going to the fridge and grabbing a beer. I crack it open and flop down onto my sofa.

The cold liquid pours down my throat and I sigh in satisfaction. I drink about half the bottle in one gulp, and then open my eyes. I stare at the beer in my hands, peeling the label off slowly.

She's pregnant.

Three or four weeks, that would put us at the Christmas party.

Is it even mine?

As soon as the thought crosses my mind I dismiss it. I know it's mine. It has to be mine! Who else's would it be? The timeline makes sense, and we never used any protection. How could I be so stupid?!

I can't believe she's pregnant. As soon as Doctor Mac said

the words I couldn't think or hear or speak. I could hardly focus on the road.

I lay back in the sofa and put a hand over my eyes. I replay the day in as much detail as I can. Harper's sickness, her hesitation about going to the doctor, telling me she'd take care of it on her own.

What if she planned this?? What if she's exactly like all the other women that I've worked so hard to avoid. I'm usually so careful! I've had so many women try to get themselves pregnant just to attach themselves to me. What if she's just another one of them?

I crack another beer open and feel the anger welling up inside me. She played me. She never told me why she knew she wouldn't get pregnant, and like a fool I just took her at her word. I assumed she was on the pill, but I never fucking asked! She's probably been trying to trap me with a kid this whole time!

She's just like the rest of them.

I bring the bottle of beer to my lips and drink another quarter of it. I churns in my stomach and feeds my anger.

I thought she was different. I was starting to care about her! I thought I was starting to—urgh—*love* her! The thought of it makes me swallow the rest of the beer. Love! What am I thinking. She's just another gold digging woman looking for an easy way out.

My thoughts come hard and fast, swirling through my head until I'm dizzy. My anger gives way to panic. I'm going to be a father! My panic gives way to uncertainty. She looked just as shocked as I was. My uncertainty turns to anger again. She's just a fucking good actor, is all.

I drink beer after beer after beer until I can't see straight and the pain in my chest dulls to an ache, and then I drink some more.

I WAKE UP AMIDST STALE, empty beer bottles. I passed out on the sofa. My cheek is glued to the leather couch and I slowly peel myself off to sit up. My head is spinning, and my mouth tastes like death.

The bottles around me tell a story. I don't usually drink this much. I don't usually drink in response to upsetting news. I'm usually able to control my emotions.

Not this time.

I groan as I stand up, walking like a zombie towards the bathroom. I turn on the shower and as it heats up I brush my teeth. I undress and stand under the hot water without moving for an eternity. I open my mouth and try to wash the taste of toothpaste and beer out of my mouth.

Last night, my mind was a torrent of thoughts and emotions and today I'm completely empty. I'm numb. I can't even string a coherent thought together. I'm on autopilot and I just let my body lead me. I get out of the shower, shave, get dressed. I head downstairs and get in the car. Before I know where I am, I'm back at the office. I was planning on taking a few days off, but the rest of the team will be back from their holidays and I have nowhere else to go. At least when I'm there I can try to forget about yesterday.

I ignore everyone as I make the long walk from the elevators to my office. I get in and close the door. I sit down and put my pounding head in my hands. I shouldn't have drank that much.

Taking a deep breath, I turn on my computer. Before I can bring myself to focus on anything work-related, my door flies open. I hear Becca protest but Rosie stomps in anyways and slams the door behind her. She balls her fists and puts them down on the desk across from me, leaning towards me. Her eyes are shooting flames at me and her nostrils flare with every breath.

"How dare you," she spits at me. I lean back. "How dare you abandon Harper like that. You fucking sack of shit!" Her voice is getting more and more strained.

"What are you talking about?"

"Oh fuck off, Zach. You're a fucking piece of shit. You find out you got a girl pregnant, one that you've been spending every waking hour with, and the next thing you do is shut down and dump her off at her house by herself?!? She's a fucking mess, Zach, and it's your fault."

Her chest is heaving and I can feel the anger hit me like a wall.

"I didn't... I don't.." I can't answer her. I try to remember what happened yesterday but it's a complete blur. My head is splitting.

"And the only thing you had to say to her," Rosie stands up, pointing a finger at my chest. "The only *fucking* thing you had to say was to ask her if she was going to *keep it*?!?! You insensitive prick! I always thought you were an asshole and you've just proven me right. I thought maybe I had you wrong when I saw how happy Harper was but you're the worst kind of man. You coward." She spits the last word at me and without waiting for me to reply she spins around and walks out. My office door slams and I jump in my seat.

I sit back in my chair and bring my hands to my temples. My head is still pounding.

I asked her if she was going to keep it?? Slowly, the memory comes back to me. We were in the car, and I was staring at the sidewalk through the windshield. Rosie's anger lifts a curtain of fog on my mind. She's right. I've been an ass. Harper needed me and I abandoned her, and made her feel like it was all a mistake.

Oh God, I am a prick. Of course she wasn't using me! Of course she wasn't faking it! What was I thinking?! I spent all day and all night feeling sorry for myself and getting drunk off my ass and I just abandoned Harper. She's pregnant and alone and probably thinks I hate her.

My heart drops. I have to fix this. With trembling hands I pick up my phone and dial her number. It goes straight to voicemail. She's either turned her phone off or blocked my number. The panic starts rising in my throat as I realise what the past twelve hours must have been like for her. I stand up and grab my coat.

I need to see her. I need to fix this.

34

HARPER

MY WHOLE BODY aches from tiredness and the raw emptiness after an emotional day. My eyes are almost swollen shut from crying so much yesterday. My whole face is puffy and blotchy.

I've hardly slept, tossing and turning all night. Rosie left this morning and now my apartment feels cold and empty. I don't know what I'd do without her. Her rage and indignation when I told her about Zach's reaction made me feel validated, but it also made the heartbreak that much more real. It's not just me, it's not in my head. He should have been better.

He should have been better, but he wasn't. He isn't the man I thought he was.

I open the fridge door and close it again. My stomach feels empty but I'm not hungry. It's like my insides have been ripped out and all that's left is a shell. I wander back to my bedroom and get under the covers. I avoid the bathroom. I don't want to look at myself right now. Bed is the only place I want to be right now.

I wonder if I could have done anything different. If I could have reacted better. I shouldn't have brought him into that doctor's room. What was I thinking?! Am I seven years old?! Why did I need to bring another person with me! I'm a grown woman!! If he hadn't been there I could have figured out a way to tell him that was better, gentler.

I sigh and turn onto my back, staring at the ceiling. Who am I kidding? If he had that much of a negative reaction, it probably doesn't matter how I told him. Rosie's voice echoes in my mind. She had her arms around me last night when she told me, *He's an ass, Harps. You're better than him. If he doesn't want to be a part of your child's life then you will figure it out. You're the strongest most determined person I know.*

I'm sick of crying but I feel the tears prickling the corners of my eyes. I rub my eyes angrily. Maybe I am strong and determined but right now I just feel scared and alone and small. How can I go back to work?! How can I face him, knowing that I'm pregnant with his child and he wants nothing to do with me. How can I face the rest of the office?! There'll be questions and I'm sure the truth will come out at some point.

I'll be the laughingstock of the whole company. I'll be ruined. All my hard work to get where I am, gone. It's a small industry, I'm sure the news that Zach Lockwood knocked up one of his employees will travel far and fast.

My cheeks burn and I feel a deep sense of shame. I don't know how to go on with my life now. I don't know how to face the world, how to go to work, how to keep going knowing I'll be raising a kid on my own. It doesn't feel like a miracle baby right now.

My hand drifts to my stomach, like it has been every few minutes since I found out I was pregnant. What if none of it matters? It doesn't matter what other people say, it doesn't matter if Zach is an asshole, it doesn't matter if my career has to change.

I'm pregnant.

I went through so much pain and heartbreak thinking it would never happen and now here I am, lamenting the fact that it did! I'm pregnant!

My heart beats harder and I sit up in bed. A smile creeps across my face for the first time since before I got the news. My head fills with images of tiny clothes, toys, holding my own child in my arms. Will it be a boy or a girl? What would I prefer? Either one is perfect, as long as it's healthy. I smile. Now I get it, when people say that. I always thought it was something that people just said to be polite, but I get it. Whatever my child is, I'm going to love it more than I've ever loved anything before.

The fire burning inside me starts to spark up again. Where I felt empty and hollow a few minutes ago I feel a love start to grow. Love for *my child*. I'm going to be a mother. The warmth grows and grows and grows until my chest feels completely full. All that matters is having a healthy, happy baby. I'll figure the rest out.

Maybe Doctor MacDonald was right, it really is a miracle baby. *My own Christmas miracle*, I think with a smile.

"I won't let anybody hurt you, ever," I whisper to my stomach. "I mean that."

I feel so full of love that I might explode. I don't need Zach, I don't need anybody. I lay back in bed and close my eyes with both hands cupping my stomach. I take a deep breath and feel myself drifting off to a deep sleep for the first time since I left Zach's apartment.

35

ZACH

HARPER HASN'T ANSWERED her phone all day. It must be turned off. I'm hoping so, anyways, because the thought of her blocking my number is driving me nuts. I might as well have taken a day off work because I haven't accomplished a thing. I'm going to have to go talk to Harper. I need to hold her in my arms and I need her to be okay with me.

"Becca," I say, pressing a button on my intercom.

Her tinny voice replies right away: "Yes, Mr. Lockwood?"

"Can you get me a bunch of nice flowers? I need them asap. Just get them brought here and I'll take them."

"Sure thing. What kind of flowers?"

I pause. I don't even know the names of any flowers except roses. A dozen red roses seems a bit too... tired? Cliche? I don't think Harper would go for roses.

"Uhh... I don't know. Pink ones. And some white ones too. Something nice and big, something that says," *sorry, I'm here for you, I'm an idiot please talk to me, of course I'll be there for you and the kid,* "I love you."

"No problem."

The phone clicks and I sit back in my chair. *I love you.* The words just fell out of my mouth so naturally even though I could have said a million different things. Do I love Harper? Did I just say that out loud?! Those aren't words that were in my vocabulary when it came to women. My mom, sure, I tell her I love her, but another woman? A romantic relationship?!

I rub my fingers over my eyes and blow the air out of my nostrils.

Of course I fucking love her.

I love her.

I've spent every waking minute either with her or wishing I was with her for the past three weeks. What else could it be? Every time I see her I get butterflies in my stomach. I didn't even know that was a thing! I thought it was just an expression that people say, but I literally feel like butterflies are crashing around my stomach when Harper turns those green eyes towards me. I can't get enough of her smell, her touch, her skin, her sex.

Is this what love is? Is it this out of control, amazing feeling that can turn to absolute shit at the drop of a hat?

I don't know if I can handle this. I stand up and stretch my arms overhead before pacing back and forth in my office. I imagine her opening the door. In my mind she's wearing a plain tank top and jeans and her hair is in a high bun over her head, exactly how she looked when she was lounging at my place.

Harper, don't close the door.

Harper, hi.

Hi, Harper.

I love you.

I stop pacing and exhale loudly. None of it sounds right!

None of it sounds good enough. How can I make her understand that I fucking love her? I would do anything for her!

I put a hand against the wall and close my eyes while I lean forward. My forehead touches the wall and I stay motionless for a few moments.

She's pregnant, and I'm going to be a father. I've basically told her that I have no interest in being involved and I abandoned her right after we both found out. How the fuck am I going to make her think that I'm not an absolute deadbeat?

My heart starts thumping in my chest. I've messed up so badly. I could have held her hand, I could have looked her in the eye. I could have said *anything*! Anything except "so you're keeping it."

A knock on the door pulls me out of my head. Becca opens the door holding a massive bouquet of pink and white flowers. I don't know how she got them so quickly.

"You're a magician," I say as I turn to her.

"That's why I get the big bucks," she responds with a grin. I make a mental note to review her salary.

Taking the flowers from her, I put my nose to them. Even these flowers remind me of Harper. They smell just as sweet as she does.

"Thanks, Becca."

"Anytime. Who's the lucky lady?"

"Just a friend," I say, not looking at her.

"Mm-hmm," she responds. The disbelief is written all over her face. I smile for the first time in forever. It feels like my face is cracking from the effort of curling my lips up.

"A good friend," I explain.

"Sure, sure," Becca says, still not changing her expression. "Anything else you'd want me to get your 'friend'? A bottle of champagne? Some chocolates? A diamond ring? You know, while we're buying friendly presents."

I laugh. "Just flowers today."

"She's a lucky lady."

I glance at Becca to see if there's any hint of sarcasm in her. She smiles at me and her eyes soften. She's telling the truth.

"I'm not so sure," I say quietly. "I think I'm the lucky one."

Becca nods and leaves the office. I put the flowers down on my desk and grab my jacket. I fidget with my clothes, my hair, I rub my face. The butterflies are back in my stomach, but this time they're flapping their wings angrily, crashing around inside me as my heart beats against my ribcage. I'm nervous.

With one last breath I grab the flowers and head out. As I'm crossing the room I see a head pop up from a cubicle. It's Rosie. She sees the flowers in my hand and one eyebrow inches up her forehead. We look at each other for a moment and she nods slowly.

I'll take that as a good sign. At least she's not yelling.

36

HARPER

I GLANCE AT MY PHONE, still sitting on the kitchen counter where I left it last night. It's completely flat, and I haven't had the heart to charge it. What if Zach has tried to call me, and what if he's mad? What if he said something awful about the baby, or about me or about getting rid of it? I don't think I'll be able to handle him being mad at me.

What if he hasn't called?

That's even worse. I look at the blank screen and feel my pulse speed up. For almost 24 hours I've been alternating between crying, sleeping, and watching TV like I'm some sort of zombie.

I grab the phone and stick it into the charger. Might as well find out where we stand. It seems to take forever to turn on. The screen lights up and then goes dark again and I sigh. It must need a few minutes to charge before I can turn it on.

Stupid phone.

The black screen stares back at me, taunting me with its uselessness. I huff and turn around. I guess a few more minutes of silence won't kill me. I start pacing up and down my living room as I wait. I'll have to call him.

Hey, Zach.

Hello Zach.

Hi.

We need to talk.

I need to talk to you.

Listen, I'm having this baby whether you like it or not!

I care about you and I'd love it if you were a part of our child's life.

Our child.

I stop walking and put my hands on my hips. I have no idea what to say to him. He was so catatonic when we got the news, so dismissive. It's like I turned into a completely different person. How could he be so callous?!

I'm not even sure I want someone like that in my life, in my baby's life! Sure, the baby's dad will be rich but do I really want someone like that around my child?! Someone who can just change their whole personality the minute they get some unexpected news?! Someone whose first instinct is to get an *abortion*???

My hand flies to my stomach again as if to reassure the baby that I'm not going to let that happen.

I glance towards the table where I left my phone and see it light up as it turns on. I'm not sure I'm ready for this.

I start walking towards it when there's a knock on the door.

Zach?

My heart starts thumping in my chest. What if he's here? What would I say?? My phone starts buzzing and beeping as it connects to the network. There's another knock on the door, more insistent this time.

I glance at the screen. I have eight missed calls and 4 messages from Zach, and two messages from Rosie. Relief floods through me. He wants to talk to me! He must be here. I glance towards the door and practically run towards it.

There's one more knock.

"Coming!" I call out.

I stand on the other side of the door. My hand is trembling as I reach for the doorknob. I put my hand on it and take a deep breath. I try to think of what I want to say but all thought has evaporated from my head. I can hardly stand up straight I'm shaking so much. I close my eyes for a second and inhale deeply. This is it.

I turn the doorknob and slide the deadbolt out. I swing the door open and feel my heart flutter in my chest.

Confusion writes itself on my face when I see the person standing at the door. It's not Zach. It's a man wearing a hoodie, facing away from the door. I frown, and the flutters in my chest turn to thumping heartbeats.

"Hello?" I hate how uncertain my voice sounds.

The man turns around slowly and I stumble backwards. Fear crawls up my spine as he smiles a toothy grin.

"Hello, Harper."

My phone rings behind me where I left it plugged into the charger on the table. I can't tear my eyes away from the man.

"Greg," I breathe. His eyes are sharp and menacing and I'm frozen to the floor. He licks his lips slowly as he watches me. A bead of sweat drips down the side of his face. We look at each other as my phone buzzes behind me.

"Your phone is ringing," he rasps.

Suddenly it's like the spell is broken. I try to slam the door but he's too fast. He sticks his boot in the doorway and shoves it open, sending me sprawling to the ground. Before I can pick myself up, he's on top of me.

I swing my arms and kick and try to scream but in an instant he has something over my mouth and nose. It's a cloth. I take a deep breath to try to scream and inhale a sickly sweet scent. Suddenly I'm dizzy, my limbs feel heavy, my eyes are blurry. Before I can stop myself I try to inhale again and everything goes dark.

37

ZACH

As I PULL up to Harper's apartment block I have to smile. I'll talk to her and hold her and fix this. She's in here and so is my kid. My kid! I've never felt anything as strong as what I feel for Harper, and now she's carrying my first child.

The doctor said it was a miracle baby—maybe he's right. It's a miracle that Harper and I found each other, it's a miracle that I let her into my life, it's a miracle that she got pregnant when she was told it was impossible.

I put the car in park and think about her face after the first time we slept together. When I asked her about birth control I'd seen such raw pain in her face, and now I know why. She thought she wasn't able to have kids. I could see the pain in her face before I took her to the doctor and now it makes sense.

I'm going to be a father. My chest heaves as I take a deep breath. Somewhere in that apartment block is an amazing woman and she's carrying my child. I can hear the blood rushing in my ears when I think about raising a kid. It's terrifying and exciting at the same time.

It's almost as terrifying as the thought of walking up those steps and facing Harper. No, not facing her. Grovelling. I'm prepared to beg, grovel, plead, do whatever I need to do to make her understand that I made a mistake.

I'll tell her I'll be there for her and the baby. I'll tell her I made a mistake. I'll tell her I reacted horribly and I'm sorry.

I'll tell her I love her.

The thought of saying those words out loud instantly makes my palms start to sweat. I've never put myself on the line like this before. There's never been more than just sex with a woman and me. The flowers that Becca chose are sitting in the passenger's seat. I grab them roughly and open the door.

This is it.

I pause when my foot hits the ground. Maybe I should warn her that I'm here. Give her a heads up so that I'm not just showing up at her door. I pull out my phone and dial her number.

It rings! She didn't block my number.

"Come on, Harper, answer!" The phone rings and rings until her voice comes on over the receiver.

"*Hi, I can't come to the phone right now. Leave a message!*"

I sigh and try her again. It rings out to voicemail again.

"Damn it!"

Her apartment building looks dark and uninviting. I shake my head. I'm just delaying this because I'm nervous. I need to just get up there and see her and explain how I feel. I climb out of my car and walk up the steps and find the door to the building propped open with a small doorstop. I push it open and look at the steps. I don't even know what apartment she's in. There's an intercom and a list of names, so I ring the number for H. Anderson.

It buzzes and buzzes without a response. I frown. I try it again with no luck. What if she isn't home? I glance up the stairway and then look at the bunch of flowers in my hand. Should I wait in my car? I spin around in a circle, uncertain of what to do. What if she's here, she's just ignoring me?

I *need* to see her. I need to tell her how I feel. I need to apologise for being an absolute ass! If she's here then I have to at least try to look into those eyes of hers and tell her the truth, that I love her and I'll do anything for her. I was in shock yesterday, but I want to be with her. I can't say that I'm ready to be a dad, but I can try.

I see a stack of old junk mail in the corner and rush over. Rifling through the old envelopes and flyers, I try to spot her name. Surely she'd have her apartment number on it?

I'm starting to lose hope when an old magazine catches my eye.

The Economist.

"Of course," I say under my breath with a grin. She's always learning. And there it is, right under her name. Apartment 407.

I roll the magazine and slip it into my jacket's breast pocket. I practically run up the stairs and by the time I make it to the fourth floor I'm panting. Don't apartment buildings have elevators these days?!

"I need to work out more," I say to myself. I glance at the wall and see the arrow pointing left for apartments 401-412. I turn down the hallway and half-walk, half-jog down.

My heart is beating faster than it was running up the stairs, which I didn't think was possible.

401, 403, 405... 407!

I skid to a stop in front of her door. Taking a few deep breaths, I try to calm my beating heart. I smooth my hair back by running my fingers through it. With one more breath and hold the flowers upright and ball my fist.

My knock sounds hollow against the door. I knock three times.

Tap-tap-tap.

No answer. I knock again.

Tap-tap-tap-tap.

Still nothing. I sigh, raising my hand one more time and slamming it against the door.

"Harper!"

I wait for two, three, four seconds but all I hear is the sound of silence. I hold my breath and try to listen for any movement inside, any indication that she's home. I can't hear a thing. I try knocking again but when no one answers my chin drops to my chest and I sigh.

She's either not here or she doesn't want to see me.

My feet felt light as a feather a few minutes ago when I was running up the steps, but now it feels like my boots are made of lead. I drag myself away from the door and make my way to the steps. At the top, I glance back down the hallway, just in case she's there waiting to run into my arms.

The empty hallway stares back at me, taunting me. I sigh and turn back to the stairs. I trudge downwards, swinging the flowers back and forth with every step. The tops of the flowers are brushing the edges of the stairs as I go down, but I don't care.

She probably wants nothing to do with me. What would a couple flowers change?

I push the front door open and walk down the steps. My mind is swirling with all kinds of thoughts about Harper, about seeing her, about apologising. I can't focus on anything and it feels like all my thoughts are rushing at me all at once.

It's not until I'm almost at my car that I see the man leaning against it. I stop in my tracks and my brow knits together as an unnerving smile paints itself across his lips. My blood runs cold as I recognise him.

"Hello, Mr. Lockwood."

"Greg Chesney," I breathe. "What the fuck are you doing here?"

38

ZACH

His eyes slide over me and I almost shiver. There's nothing in them—no emotion, no anger, no fear. He's completely dead behind the eyes. He makes me just as uncomfortable as he did at the Christmas party.

"What are you doing here?"

He holds up his hand and something glints. I frown, but stay rooted in place. I don't want to get any closer, and I'd prefer it if he stopped leaning against my car. I'd prefer it if he disappeared forever and never came anywhere near me or Harper, but that doesn't seem to be happening.

"I could ask you the same thing. I told you to stay away," he growls as he holds up the item a little bit higher. I stare at it until I finally realise what it is.

"Harper's ring."

"Harper's ring!" He shouts. "That I gave to *you* as a warning, and now I find it on her finger?!"

"So it was you who sent it to me," I say.

"Harper and I belong together. Everyone wants to tear us apart but I won't let that happen. We belong together."

His chest is heaving up and down as he stares at me, his eyes darting back and forth. He's obsessed with her. Does he know about the baby? The thought of this man being anywhere near Harper and my child makes my blood turn to ice.

"Where's Harper?"

"She's at home," he replies. An eery grin appears on his face. "She's in bed!"

His face terrifies me. Harper is in danger. My heart starts pounding in my chest and I try to reach into my pocket slowly. I need to call the police.

"I swear to God, Greg, if you touched one hair on her fucking head I'll kill you myself," I growl.

Greg ignores me. "I told you to stay away from her. We belong together. You people keep trying to tear us apart!" His eyes are becoming wilder with every second.

"Who's trying to tear you apart?"

"You, stealing her away from me. That bitch Rosie always whispering in her ear about me, poisoning Harper's mind. You all just want to keep us away from each other. We belong together."

"She doesn't want to be with you," I say as calmly as I can manage. My whole body is trembling. My fingers have found my phone in my pocket but I can't remember how to dial emergency without looking at it.

"You're lying!" He yells as he pushes himself off the car, taking a step towards me. I put my hand up defensively, flowers in one hand and phone in the other.

"Stay back."

"Or what," he snarls. "I warned you. I warned you to stay away from her."

"Since when do you have jurisdiction over Harper? Since you fucking terrorised her last year?"

"Terrorised her!?" His eyes widen and I see they're not dead anymore. They're alive with fury. "I terrorised her?? It was that bitch Rosie, I just told you. She twisted Harper's mind and made her hate me. She was going to be my girlfriend! We were going to get married!"

I say nothing as I watch the spit flying out of his mouth with every word. He doesn't bother to wipe it off his lips where it lands, only stares at me as he thrusts Harper's ring towards me.

"And now Rosie has poisoned you too. She's convinced you to go after Harper just to take her away from me."

I feel my brows knit together. Rosie? Why does he have such a vendetta against her?

"Rosie has nothing to do with this," I say, trying to keep my voice steady.

"Rosie has everything to do with this!" He yells. He takes another step towards me and puts the ring into his pocket and then reaches for something in the same pocket. My blood is thick in my veins as I watch him. I hold up the flowers defensively and wish I had something better to protect myself with. Finally I'm able to press the emergency button on my phone before slipping it back into my pocket. I keep my eyes on Greg.

"Where's Harper?"

"She doesn't want to see you."

"That's not what I asked, Greg. Where is she?"

"I said she doesn't want to see you!"

His eyes are practically popping out of his head. The veins on his neck are pulsing with every heartbeat and his chest is heaving up and down. His eyes are darting back and forth from me to the stairs to the street. I want to do the same, to look around and see what my options are but I can't risk looking away from him. He's completely unpredictable. Why is there no one on this street?! Usually New York has throngs of people and now it's deserted??

Greg Chesney looks back at me. His hand is still in his pocket and his eyes get darker.

"I saw you," he says. His voice passes through my chest and makes my whole body grow colder. "I saw you at the Christmas party. You stole her from me."

"She came to me," I say, my hands still up. "She came to me."

"She would never do that! She's pure. She's *mine*."

He lunges towards me, finally pulling his hand out of his pocket. I see a glint of steel as he rushes towards me, just seeing the knife come down on my chest at the last moment. His body collides with mine and I fall backwards. Pain shoots through my chest and I feel the knife press into my flesh like a hot blade through butter.

Greg's eyes are inches from mine and feel his breath on my face like hot garbage. I try to push him off but I can't move my arm. Suddenly everything feels heavy and I see a dark puddle growing next to me. It looks black until my eyes adjust a second later.

Blood.

My blood.

The last thing I see is Greg's arm coming down on my face and sending an explosion of pain through my temple.

39

HARPER

MY HEAD IS SPLITTING. It's like there's an ax buried deep in my skull right across my forehead, and the rest of my head is shattered in a million pieces. A groan escapes my lips and I try to open my eyes.

I'm in my own bed.

Any relief I feel quickly evaporates when I try to move. My hands and legs are bound with rope, keeping me spread eagle over my bed. My heart jumps against my ribcage and the panic starts clouding my vision. I struggle against my restraints but I can hardly even move my wrists more than an inch or so across.

Greg Chesney.

I force my eyes open wider even though the dim winter sunlight makes my entire head ache. I glance around the room, whipping my head back and forth to see if he's here. He must be here, who else would have tied me up like this?! I glance down and feel a small drop of relief when I see I'm still fully clothed. There's that, at least.

I whimper and then I hear a sound just outside my

window. The old window slides up with a loud scrape and Greg's face peers in through the opening.

"You're up!" He says cheerily. I don't answer. The cold breeze hits me and I shiver. He climbs in through the window and closes it behind him. Why is he using the fire escape?

"I didn't want to disturb you so I went out for some coffee. He produces two steaming mugs, holding them up proudly. "You look so peaceful when you sleep."

His eyes are wild. He comes closer and I can smell the familiar odour of wet socks and staleness that follows him like a cloud. I try not to shudder.

"Did you have a good snooze?"

His pleasantness is almost more disturbing than if he were menacing right now. I don't know how to react. His eyes are darting around the room and he takes another step towards me, holding the coffee out. His jacket is stained in the front and on the sleeve, a dark brown patch as if he spilled coffee all over himself.

He gets closer still and I stare at the stain. The edges look almost red. My eyes widen and I look up at his face.

It's blood. My already wild heart jumps again and my throat starts to close. I can't breathe. Whose blood is that?! Is it mine? Is it his?? Is it someone else's?!!

Greg notices my gaze and makes a noise almost like a growl. He puts the coffee down on the bedside table and rips his jacket off.

"What are you looking at?" He barks. He throws the jacket off to the side and it lands with a thud. I can still see it and the bloodstain from where I'm lying. I shift my gaze back to Greg. He's standing over me with his hands on his hips, as if he's deciding what he wants to do.

I'm completely powerless. I can't move and the panic is

making it impossible for me to speak. I can hardly even breathe.

"You're very quiet today, puppet," he says, taking a seat next to me. His gnarled, dirty finger reaches towards my face and I turn away, squeezing my eyes shut. He strokes the side of my face with his finger, tracing the line of my jaw all the way down my neck. I keep my eyes shut and hold my breath until it's over.

"You're shaking! Are you cold?" There's concern in his voice. I open my eyes and watch as he gets a blanket from the cupboard and throws it over me. "There."

His hair is sticking up in all directions and his eyes are hazy and unfocused. He won't look at something for more than a second, and his movements are sharp and jittery. He sits down on the bed again.

"Oh! I almost forgot your coffee. Here," he presents it to me as if he doesn't realise my arms and legs are bound.

"I.. I can't," I finally say, nodding towards my hands.

"Oh of course," he replies. He leans in towards me and another wave of stench invades my nostrils. His greasy hand cups the back of my head. Is that blood under his fingernails?

He lifts my head almost gently and brings the coffee cup to my lips.

"Careful! It's hot!" He says with a child-like giggle. I take a sip and nod.

"Thanks," I respond. He smiles, satisfied, and puts the coffee back on the table. He folds his hand in his lap and looks at me. It looks almost like his smile is plastered on his face but the rest of his features didn't follow along. It's like his eyes operate on a completely different circuit than the rest of his face.

"Great. Now, what should we do? Do you want to play

cards? I remember you said you were great at Blackjack! Have you got any cards?"

I take a deep breath. "Greg, what's going on? What are you doing here?"

"What do you mean, puppet? We're together, finally. This is how it's meant to be. Everyone else is out of the way and now we can finally be the way we're supposed to be."

My blood turns to ice. *Everyone else is out of the way?*

"Greg, we're not together. I'm your boss."

"That didn't stop you a couple weeks ago, did it!" His head spins towards me and the spittle flies off his lips as he almost shouts the words at me. He leans towards me and my whole body goes rigid. The ropes at my wrists and ankles digs into my skin but I can't relax my body enough to ease the pain, not when Greg's face is inches from mine and he's breathing heavily. His eyes are completely dark.

He knows. He saw us. I knew there was someone. My stomach drops as I realise I should have listened to my instincts. Greg sits up again and his feature rearrange themselves again. He smiles at me.

"That's okay," he says, patting my arm. "We're together now and that's all that matters. Wouldn't you agree?"

"Yeah," I say quickly.

"Say you agree," he says.

"I agree."

Greg nods and gets up, brushing his hands together. "I hope you're hungry, I've been planning our first meal together for over a year! I learned to cook from my grandmother," he explains. "I'm quite the expert with a knife!"

My eyes shoot back to the jacket on the ground, and the bloodstain down the front. *Expert with a knife* echoes in my brain over and over and over.

40

ZACH

"Sir, you're at the hospital. You've been stabbed but we're going to stitch you up. Everything is going to be fine."

There's a voice near my left ear and it keeps telling me things. *You're going to be okay.* I feel like I'm moving and my eyes flutter open. The ceiling is rushing past me. I try to move my head but there's something around my neck. Thick straps are holding me down to the bed.

"Get him to OR-B, it's been prepped and the surgeon is ready. What's his status?"

"Lost a lot of blood. Stabbed about an inch below the heart. If he hadn't had a magazine in his pocket he wouldn't be here right now."

"Lucky."

"Definitely."

"Any ID?"

"In his wallet. Zachary Lockwood, 37 years old. No medical details. Called from his cell phone and found him alone on the street."

Doors swing open and my bed rolls down another white

hallway. *Stabbed. Lost a lot of blood.* I try to process the words as they reach my ears but I can't make sense of anything. A new voice comes close to my ear again, a woman.

"Zachary, we're going to operate on your chest. We need to sew you back up and get you healthy again, okay? You're going to be fine."

Why do they keep telling me I'll be fine? Lights are flashing by on the ceiling as the bed rolls forward. I try to speak but all that comes out is a gurgled groan. There's something in my mouth. Harper! I need to tell them about Harper! She's in danger!

"Don't speak, Zachary. You've been intubated. We're going to fix you right up in no time."

I'm wheeled into a room and I see multiple bodies around my bed. They count together and suddenly I'm lifted onto a hard surface. More voices, more movement. I try to catch their attention. I need to tell them about Harper! There's no time. They're telling me something and then I feel like the blood in my arm has turned to ice. The cold feeling travels up my arm and then I'm asleep.

"I THINK HE'S WAKING UP," a low voice says. I open my eyes and squint. I try to move my head but everything hurts. My throat is on fire. My vision clears and I see a familiar face next to the bed.

"Mitch?"

"Hey, buddy. You gave us quite the scare. How are you feeling?"

"Horrible. Where am I?"

"You're at the hospital. You were stabbed. What happened?"

I groan. One by one, the memories start coming back to me. Harper's apartment. The blood spreading around me. The feeling of the knife sinking into my chest. Greg Chesney's face just inches away from mine.

"I was stabbed," I explain. *Harper!* My pulse jumps up.

Mitch chuckles. "Yeah, we gathered that. I mean what happened that led to you getting stabbed? Why were you over there anyways, that's nowhere near your apartment."

There's a noise to my right and I turn my head slowly. Two police officers come into the room in full uniform.

"Mr Lockwood," the burly man in front says. He's clearly in charge. "My name is Officer Benson. This is Officer Green." He nods to his partner. "We'd like to ask you a few questions."

I nod. Even that slight movement makes the pain shoot down my spine.

"Do you know the person who stabbed you?"

"Greg," I try to speak but my throat is too hoarse. "Greg Chesney. You need to get him. He's dangerous!"

The officer jots down the name. "And who is Greg Chesney? How do you know him?"

"He works for me. Used to work for me."

"What were you doing when he stabbed you?"

"Trying to go see my girlfriend." The word comes naturally. I hear Mitch make a noise but I ignore him. She's my girlfriend, and she's in trouble. "He's obsessed with her. He was stalking her last year and nobody ever did anything to it. He threatened me and then stabbed me. You need to find him. She's in trouble. He said she was in her apartment in bed but I couldn't get in. That's when he stabbed me. You need to go! There's no time!"

"Okay, sir, calm down," Officer Benson says in a stern voice. "Can you describe Greg Chesney for us?"

I give them the best description I can and tell them what happened. They nod and write things down.

"Okay, thank you. If you remember anything else just call this number." He leaves a card on the table next to me. They turn to leave and I make a noise.

"Officer?"

He turns to look at me, waiting for me to speak.

"She's pregnant." I say. "Harper is pregnant. Please find her." The two officers exchange a glance and then look at me.

"We'll find her," he says with certainty before turning around and leaving.

I lie back in bed and close my eyes. Mitch clears his throat.

"So... were you ever going to tell me that you and Harper were.. together. And that you knocked her up?!"

"Just shut up, Mitch, please," I say without opening my eyes. "It's been a rough couple days."

He says nothing and I open my eyes to look at him. His eyes are wide and he's staring at me in disbelief. I try to grin but my face won't let me.

"You're looking at me like I'm from outer space," I croak.

"You might be," he replies with a laugh. "What the fuck, man! I don't even know you."

"I don't know, Mitch. It's been a crazy couple weeks. There's something about her." I try to sit up and wince as the pain shoots through my chest. "I've never met a woman like her before. They have to find her. *I* have to find her!"

"You're going nowhere," Mitch says sternly. "If I have to sit here and babysit you I will. Let the police do their job."

"Mitch, you don't understand. She thinks I hate her. She thinks I don't want the baby. I have to find her and make it right."

"They'll find her, and you can tell her that yourself when they do. Zach, look at yourself," Mitch says. "You look like hell, and you've got tubes sticking out all over the place. You can barely move without wincing. Let the police do their job. You just got fucking stabbed in the heart!"

I lie back on the bed and close my eyes. He's right, I can hardly move. As much as I hate it, I won't be able to get out of this bed. My heart has been through a lot these past couple days. I try to relax but all I can think of is Harper. They need to find her. She needs to be safe.

Mitch puts a hand on my arm as if he can sense my panic. "It'll be okay," he says in a low voice. "It'll be okay."

41

HARPER

"I JUST HAVE one more thing to take care of, and then we can be together forever, puppet." Greg is putting on his jacket and heading for the fire escape. "You just sit tight, I'll be right back."

"What are you going to take care of?" I ask.

"Rosie."

Before I can respond, he's out the window and slams it shut. The noise of the window coming down on the frame vibrates through my chest and I yell in panic. Greg looks at me through the closed window and grins before spinning around and disappearing down the fire escape.

His face stays etched in my vision, the toothy smile of a madman staring at me through the window. My breath is shallow.

Rosie.

He's going to *take care of her*?! What does that even mean?? He seems to think that she's the one who stopped us being together, not the fact that he's a stalker that I had no interest in being with. I need to get out of here. I need to protect Rosie! I need to protect myself!!

I struggle against my bonds once again. It's no use. He has them tied up in multiple knots, spreading me out so I can't get any leverage. I can't even move, let alone try to free myself. I relax and then yank at my arms, as if to surprise the ropes into letting me go.

Unsurprisingly, it doesn't work. Tears of frustration start welling up in my eyes. I don't have much time. I need to warn Rosie! I don't even know what he's planning on doing, but judging by the bloodstain on his jacket and the unhinged look in his eye, I can guess it's nothing good. He's dangerous, and I'm stuck here with no way of even moving more than a couple inches.

I'm starting to lose hope. I can't move these ropes at all. I'm stuck in my own home, unable to call for help and unable to set myself free. The tears are streaming down my face now. *Rosie.* My best friend, the voice of reason, the one who can make me laugh.

I can't take it. The pain grows like a ball of flame in my stomach until I have to let it out somehow.

"Help!" I scream into the void. "Help me! Someone! Please!" I scream and scream until my voice goes hoarse, and then I scream some more. I watch as the minutes tick by on my alarm clock, taunting me as my imagination runs wild with what Greg might be doing.

It takes half an hour to get to Rosie's house from here, assuming Greg is driving. That means he'll be getting there in just a few minutes. She's probably making dinner, she always eats at home. My heart starts thumping as the clocks marches on and on.

"Help!"

My voice is getting weaker and I sob. It's no use.

Just then, I hear a thump at the front door, and some muffled voices. My heart leaps.

"Help! In here!" I scream as loud as I can. My vocal cords are raw, and each sound they make sends pain through my throat. I don't care, it doesn't matter. "Help!"

The door burst open and I hear heavy footsteps.

"Police!"

"In here!" I yell. A flood of officers comes through my bedroom door and in an instant my arms and legs are free. A thousand and one questions are flying at me.

"He's gone, he's gone to Rosie's," I pant. "I know where he is! He's gone to Rosie's. I'm fine!" I shout as someone tries to tell me I need to go to the hospital. "I need to go to Rosie's!"

"You can show us the way," a large officer with a mop of curly brown hair says to me. "Green, get her in the car. We're going."

On the way out the door I grab my phone and rush down the stairways. Before I know what's happening I'm loaded into a police car and the sirens are blaring. We're flying down the roads as cars pull over left and right to let us through. I've never been in a police car and the feeling would be exhilarating if I wasn't terrified for Rosie.

There's no answer as I call Rosie over and over and over again.

"Come on, answer," I whisper to myself. "Answer!" I call her one more time and then mash the keyboard as I send her a text.

Harper: Get out of your apartment. Go somewhere safe. Call me now!

Rosie's silence is deafening and the dread is quickly overwhelming me. I rub at my wrists where the ropes left red raw marks. I know my eyes are wide and my body is completely tense as I watch us speed through red lights, green lights, around corners, through stop signs. We fly down the roads towards Rosie, but it still seems too slow.

I can't stop glancing at the clock. Time is still laughing at me, barreling on way too quickly. Surely Greg has made it to Rosie's house now. We're too late. He's already there. My mind starts to run away with thoughts of what we'll find: more dark reddish brown blood stains, Rosie, Greg, maybe he'll be gone and we'll just find Rosie.

My phone rings and I almost jump out of my seat. I look at the screen and sigh. It's not Rosie.

Zach's name flashes on the screen and my thumb hesitates over the buttons. Finally I let it press down over the one on the left: *Ignore*. I don't have time for this right now, and I definitely don't have the energy. My hand hovers over my stomach and I close my eyes. *It's okay, little buddy. We're going to be okay. I love you.*

I'm not sure if it's normal for women to talk to their foetuses like this but it gives me an ounce of comfort to know I'm not alone.

I focus on the sound of the sirens to drown out my spiralling thoughts. As the cars split on the road in front of us I shift my thinking. We're going to make it. We're nearly there. He couldn't have gotten here that fast. He'll want to draw out his punishment of Rosie, surely. We'll have time. We can make it.

We have to make it.

42

ZACH

"She hung up," I say with a sigh, tossing my phone to the side. Mitch purses his lips.

"I'm sure it's fine, the police were on their way over there. Did it go straight to voicemail?"

"Nah, it rang a couple times and then she hung up." I glance at Mitch and see him nod. He tries to keep his face straight but I know he's thinking exactly the same thing as me: That's not a good sign.

Either she can't talk, or Greg has her phone. If he saw my name flash on the screen it might have made him angry.

"What if he has her phone," I say slowly. "It might set him off to see me calling. If he has her, and he's mad..." I stare at the dark screen of my phone. My chest suddenly feels hollow at the thought that I'm endangering Harper just by calling her.

"Don't think like that. The police have been gone an hour. They're with her, they have to be. Maybe one of them hung up the phone. Maybe she can't talk because they're interviewing her. There could be a thousand things going on. Don't panic."

I nod, but I can't look at him. He could give me a thousand logical explanations but I can't stop thinking of Greg's face when it was inches from mine. His eyes were two black circles with white showing all around. There was no life in them, no emotion except rage. Rage directed at *me*. If that rage were to be aimed at Harper...

"He told me to stay away. If he sees my name on her phone he knows I'm not listening."

"Zach, stop. This isn't you. You're not like this. Don't panic. Are you in pain? Do you need more meds? Is it time for more morphine?"

I grin and finally meet Mitch's eye. "Always trying to get me fucked up, hey?"

"What else are friends for? Give me some of that IV if you're not enjoying it."

I chuckle and the movement sends pain radiating through my chest. I wince, bringing a hand up to my bandage.

"At least you'll end up with a gnarly scar," Mitch says, motioning to my chest. "The ladies love scars."

"I'm not interested in what the ladies love," I reply. I close my eyes and can almost feel Harper's fingers trail over and back across my chest. I love the way she brushes her fingertips ever so gently on my skin. It makes me feel like there's nowhere else in the world I'd rather be than right beside her.

Right now, there isn't. I try to shift my weight and groan. Even lifting my torso up away from the bed is exhausting.

"Will you stop fucking moving?! Zach, you've been stabbed! You just had major surgery." Mitch puts his hand on my shoulder. I look over at him and see the concern in his eyes. "Jesus Christ, Zach. Come on."

I nod and lay back, resigning myself to the fact that I'm going to have to let the police do their job.

Mitch sees me settle down and sits back in his chair. I sigh and close my eyes, trying to imagine Harper's eyes when she's laughing. They sparkle like two emeralds.

"So how did this all happen, you and Harper?"

I open my eyes and see Mitch staring at me curiously. His voice is casual but his eyes betray his intense curiosity. I shrug, and then wince as the pain shoots through my arm.

"It just kind of... happened. I don't know. I'd never really spoken to her and then we started spending time together at work on the Latif file and Mitch," I pause and glance at him. "She's fucking amazing. She's so smart and driven and people love her! She has the most amazing eyes and she's funny, you know? Like really funny. The things she says are just constantly surprising me."

Mitch grins. "You've got it bad. It's over. You're done."

I blow the air out of my nostrils. "I know."

"And the kid... was that planned?"

"No." I grimace. "I reacted badly. I didn't mean to."

"You said that." Mitch leans forward. "Listen, it'll work out. She'll understand. Right now you just need to focus on resting. At the end of the day you got stabbed on your way to her place. That's got to count for something, right? Like, sure, you acted like a dick when you found out but then you almost died! She can't hate you forever!"

I can't help but laugh even though I know it'll send flames of pain through my side. Mitch grins.

"Yeah, it's got to count for something."

"Let's get you some more painkillers," Mitch says as he grabs the call button next to the bed. "You deserve it."

"You're an idiot," I laugh as a nurse pops her head in the door. I lay back in bed and close my eyes. I'm glad Mitch is here, if only to distract me from the gnawing fear that I was too late, that I've put Harper in more danger, that I've ruined everything. I should have been with her.

At the end of the day he's right, I can't even move out of this bed, let alone go after a deranged stalker. I need to trust the police. If Harper and I make it out of this then I can explain myself. I can be a dad and I can be with Harper. I glance at my phone and feel another kind of pain in my chest when the blank screen stares back at me. I resist the urge to dial her number again.

43

HARPER

THE SECOND THE car stops it's a flurry of frantic activity.

"Stay here," Officer Benson commands.

"But!"

"Stay. Here." He tells me. He motions for me to put my foot back inside the car and then closes the door. He jogs up the few steps to the apartment block and I watch in frustration from my seat in the police cruiser.

I crack the door open to see if I can hear anything, and then step out of the car. There's a few police officers at the door and they motion at me to stop. I hold up my arms and motion to the car, leaning against it. *I'm not moving, I'm just going to go crazy if I have to sit in the car!* They seem to understand and turn back towards the door. I can hear the static of their radios buzzing with unintelligible voices. I wish I could hear.

I scan the building. Rosie lives in an old brick building, kind of like mine. The alleyways that surround it are narrow and dark, and I know she has a fire escape just like mine. I frown. Greg never used my front door, always choosing the fire escape. Suddenly I'm standing up like a bolt and jogging towards the officers.

"He'll use the fire escape."

"Ma'am, please go back to the car. Back up. Ma'am"

"He'll use the fire escape! We need to cover the back!"

They're not listening. One of them is grabbing my arm and guiding me towards Benson's cruiser. I yank my arm away and take off running towards the alley. Their shouts are drowned out by the pounding of my heart in my ears.

I can only hear my breath, my heartbeat, and the sound of my footsteps on the pavement. I think someone is following me and shouting but I can't be sure. I dive down the alley and sprint to the end. The fire escapes are all on the far side.

In a few steps I've reached the corner of the building. I skid around the corner, almost losing my balance as my eyes scan up the building.

I hear him before I see him. The steel staircases are clanging as he sprints down them. I glance up further and see two police officers who are at least three storeys higher than him. They'll never catch him. I scan the alleyway and see a dumpster a few feet away from me. I crouch down behind it, praying Greg won't look down and see me before he's on the ground.

If he goes the other direction I'll never get to him. The last staircase is facing me, so I'm hoping he just takes off running straight ahead.

Time seems to slow down. All day today each second seemed to rush by but now it seems like an eternity since I've been crouched behind this smelly dumpster.

I can hear Greg's footsteps. *Clang, clang, clang.* He's practically sprinting down the stairs. I can hear his breath now, ragged and laboured as he moves closer and closer. Finally I hear the crunch of gravel under his feet.

My body is like a coiled spring. I can feel every atom in my body vibrating with anticipation as each footstep brings Greg Chesney closer to my hiding spot.

One,

Two,

Three!

I didn't know it was possible for me to spring forward that quickly. The instant Greg's sprinting form passes by me I'm on his heels, rushing at him. I realise when he turns his head towards me that I'm screaming like a deranged banshee. The wordless scream rips through my raw vocal chords as I hurl myself towards him.

Our bodies crash together and I wrap my arms around him. We fall to the ground and my arm stays pinned underneath him. We land with a thud and the air gets knocked out of me. He's kicking, I'm kicking, we're flailing on the ground. My arms are around him like a vice. There's no thought, no intention, just pure animal instinct. I hear myself screaming and screaming and screaming.

Arms and legs appear around us. I'm torn off him and he's tackled to the ground again. He's handcuffed, I'm being sat down, there's screaming, movement, questions, noise.

My chest is heaving and finally I can focus my eyes. Officer Benson is leaning down, nose to nose with me.

"What the fuck were you thinking! Didn't I tell you to stay put?!"

"Rosie."

I'm panting, I can't speak. The anger in his eyes softens ever so slightly.

"Paramedics are on the way. We need to get her to hospital."

I spring up to my feet and feel his strong arms hold me back.

"Calm down, fuck!" He shouts. "Guys!" Two more sets of arms wrap themselves around me and I stop moving. "The paramedics are on the way, I said! There's nothing you can do. Come on."

He nods his head and the two men lead me out front. We turn the corner just as the ambulance skids to a stop. I resist the urge to rush forward, instead waiting in tortuously long wait until I see the stretcher come down the stairs. I push my way into the ambulance behind her. The paramedics look at me curiously but nod to the officers, who let me go.

"Rosie!"

"Harps," she pants. There's red blood seeping through the bandages the paramedics have wrapped around her stomach. "Hey."

"Shh," I say as the tears well up. I find her hand and give it a squeeze. She squeezes back weakly, and her eyes flutter closed.

"Okay, Rosie, I need you to stay with us. Stay with us, okay?" The paramedic keeps talking, keeps Rosie awake as the ambulance starts speeding down the road. I hold her hand and ignore the tears as they keep streaming down my cheeks.

"Come on, Rosie," I whisper. She squeezes my hand ever so gently and I let the tears flow down. "Come on, Rosie."

44

ZACH

My body is screaming as I lift myself off the bed. Pain is radiating from my chest through my side and down my arm. Mitch holds me steady and guides me to the wheelchair.

"This is stupid, Zach. I can go get her! You should be in bed."

"I need to see her."

There's no hesitation in my voice, and it leaves no room for argument. Mitch sighs audibly but helps me up. I blow the air out of my nostrils as soon as I'm settled in the chair. Closing my eyes, I take a deep breath as the pain in my chest dulls slightly.

"You alright?"

"Yeah, I'm fine," I respond with a grimace. I'm not fine, but I have to see her. The police told me that Harper was okay, she was here with Rosie. I didn't understand anything they said after that, something about surgery, critical condition, arrests. All I know is that Harper is in this hospital, waiting on Rosie to get out of surgery and I need to be with her.

I already messed up once by not being with her when she needed me, I'm not going to let that happen again. Mitch throws a blanket over my legs and tucks it in beside me.

"You're going to make a great mother someday, you know that Mitch?"

"Shut up, Zach," he replies with a grin. "You ready?"

"Let's go."

Mitch moves behind me and starts pushing the wheelchair. A second later, the front wheel crashes into the corner of the bed and my body lunches forward. I grunt as the impact sends another wave of nauseating pain through my chest.

"Fuck!"

"Oops! Sorry buddy!"

"Be careful! I just got stabbed for fuck's sake." I glance behind me and Mitch is looking at the doorway. I hear her before I see her.

"You two are like the Stooges," she says. I can hear the smile in her voice. "Where are you going in your state anyways?"

She's gorgeous. Harper is standing in the doorway looking radiant. Her hair is pulled back in a low bun and her eyes look tired and drawn but they're shining bright, just like I've been imagining this whole time.

"Harper," I breathe. The seconds tick by until Mitch clears his throat.

"I'll be just outside if you need me." He squeezes my shoulder as he walks by and we exchange a glance. I dip my chin down and he does the same. *Thanks,* I tell him with my eyes. The door closes softly behind him and then Harper and I are alone.

"I was just coming to find you," I say to fill the silence.

"In your state?! You fool." She's smiling and I feel the corners of my lips curl upwards.

"Maybe I am a fool. I had to see you, to make sure you were okay. Harper, I..." my voice catches in my throat. "I just want to say I'm so—"

"Stop." She holds up a hand and comes closer. Taking a seat in the chair next to the bed, she reaches forward and places her hand over mine. The second her skin touches mine, a healing warmth fills me. My throat feels like it's completely closed up. "How's your chest? They told me you were stabbed."

"It's fine," I lie. "How about you, are you okay? How's the baby?"

Harper's eyes shine bright for a second before she answers. "I'm fine. The baby is fine as well, they gave me a full checkup when I came in. I was lucky. Rosie is in bad shape. She's stable now, they're saying she'll make a full recovery. It's all my fault, for both of you! You never would have gotten hurt if you hadn't been seeing me. Greg attacked her with a knife and—"

Her voice catches and the tears fall down her cheeks. I grab her hand in mine and give it a squeeze. I notice the red marks on her wrists and brush them lightly.

"What's this?" I whisper. Harper pulls her hand away and pulls her sleeve down before brushing her tears away.

"Nothing."

"Harper.."

We stare at each other in silence until I clear my throat. "None of this is your fault, you hear me? No one could have predicted it."

I don't know what to say. I don't know where to start or how to explain how I feel. How can I put it into words? How can I tell her that she means the world to me and that I'd let myself get stabbed a million times if it meant she and our baby were safe and healthy. How can I tell her that the past couple days have been torture, not only because of Greg Chesney but because I wasn't with her, because I let her down?

I turn the wheelchair towards her and put both my hands on her knees. Finally I build up the courage to say the only thing that even comes close to describing how I feel. It comes out as a barely audible whisper as I force myself to look into her shining eyes.

"I love you."

Harper says nothing, but the tears start streaming down her cheeks again. My heart starts thumping and I reach up to brush them away.

"It's true, Harper. I love you. I'm sorry I was an ass. I want to be with you and I want to have this baby."

I can't say anything else because Harper's lips are on mine. She flies into my arms and my chest explodes, but the pain is like background noise. The only thing that matters is Harper's kiss, her touch, her body. I tangle my fingers into her hair and pull her in. This kiss is more than just a kiss. It's the end of everything that's been going on between us since that doctor's appointment. It's everything I've been too scared to say, everything I've been too scared to feel.

Harper wraps her arms around my neck and sits down on my lap. I wrap my arms around her and pull her in closer, breathing in deeply to inhale her scent. I pull my head back.

"I was so worried about you. It was killing me to be stuck here."

"I didn't think of you at all," she replies with a grin before leaning over and kissing me softly. She pulls her lips away and rests her forehead against mine. "I thought of you constantly ever since you dropped me off. Zach," she hesitates and then takes a deep breath. "I love you too."

It might have taken a few minutes for her to say it back to me but it doesn't matter. As soon as the words leave my lips I feel like I'm floating. The pain leaves my body and I run my fingers along her jaw to pull her in for another kiss.

Nothing else matters. Nothing matters except Harper and our child. I slide my hand down and place it over her stomach. She interlaces her fingers over mine and pulls her head back, smiling at me. We both look down at our hands and then back at each other's eyes. Her green eyes look like the emeralds I've been picturing all day. There's nothing in them except relief, happiness, and love.

45

HARPER

"Is this the invalid party room?" Rosie says as I wheel Zach into her room. "Who else do we know that's been stabbed?"

I laugh. "Something like that. Does that mean I'm not invited?"

"I'll make an exception for you this time," Rosie says. I smile as I push Zach over and pull up a chair beside her. Rosie looks worn out. There are dark circles under her eyes and she's got a tube of oxygen in her nose. There's an IV dripping clear liquid into her hand.

"How are you feeling?" I know it's a silly question, but I can't think of anything else to say.

"Awful," Rosie says with a grimace. "But I'll live."

"This is all my fault. I'm sorry."

Both Rosie and Zach make a noise in protest. Zach puts a hand over my arm and Rosie squeezes my hand.

"You did nothing wrong, Harps," Rosie says. "We knew he was deranged."

"If anything, it's my fault," Zach says slowly. I turn my head and see the pain in his eyes. "I didn't bother to know what was going on in my own company. I should have known what was happening a year ago, I never would have let it go on like it did. I should have been there with you when he showed up. I'm sorry."

"Will both of you stop it," Rosie says with an exaggerated sigh. "It's nobody's fault except Greg's. Did you come to my house and stab me six times?" She looks at me. "No? How about you? Did you do it?" She looks at Zach. "Right. That's what I thought. It was Greg Fucking Chesney. Now both of you need to stop beating yourselves up. We're all here, we're alive, and the baby is okay. That's all that matters."

Rosie lies back in bed and closes her eyes for a minute as if to say, *that's the end of that discussion.*

"Maybe you're right," I respond. She snorts. "Still, I wish you hadn't been stabbed."

Rosie grins, her eyes still closed. "At least I get to enjoy the best food that the hospital has to offer. And I'll have some cool scars."

I glance at Zach and he nods. I take a deep breath. For some reason I'm more nervous about this than I thought I would be.

"Rosie," I start. She makes a noise but doesn't open her eyes. "Zach and I were talking and..." I hesitate. "Will you be the baby's godmother? You're my best friend and you've always been there for me. I'd love it if you were part of my—our—kid's life as well."

Rosie finally opens her eyes and turns her head. They're misty and wet and she smiles weakly. "Of course," she whispers. "I'd be honoured."

Warmth floods through my chest I reach over and hold Rosie's hand. Zach puts his arm around my shoulders and the three of us sit there in silence. A peacefulness settles over us as we share a quiet moment. Rosie breaks the silence.

"Your kid better not be a little shit. If it's annoying you're going to hear about it."

"I never knew you were so nurturing, Rosie," Zach quips.

I laugh. "She's definitely got the Mother Hen gene."

Rosie smiles and shrugs. "I'm just telling it like it is."

We spend a few more minutes talking about nothing and everything, talking about anything except what we've just been through. I watch as both Rosie and Zach wince whenever they move and it's as is I can feel their pain in my own body. The two people I love the most have been hurt because of me. No matter how much they tell me it wasn't my fault I still feel responsible.

I fiddle with my grandmother's ring, turning it around and back on my finger. This is the ring that enraged Greg. The ring that made him stab Zach, the ring that was proof in his eyes of my connection to him. Now I know that he took it from my office, he used it to threaten Zach. He took it off my finger when I was unconscious and used it as a threat again, as proof of our indiscretions.

Zach slips his hand into mine and stops me fidgeting with the ring. I glance at him and he smiles sadly. He knows what I'm thinking, I don't need any words to know it. Rosie clears her throat.

"Alright, lovebirds. I'm getting tired and the nurse will be here soon to change my bandages. Party's over, I'm afraid."

I smile and lean over to give her a one-armed hug. She pats my back gently.

"I'll be back tomorrow, okay Rosie?"

"Just take care of yourself and the kid," she says. She

smiles and I see once again the kindness and strength that makes her who she is.

I push the wheelchair out the door and down the hallway. Zach reaches his hand up towards me and interlaces his fingers with mine. Even that simple touch calms me down. We're passed words, passed explanations. We both know that I'm his, and he's mine.

EPILOGUE

HARPER

Four months later...

"Zach! Zach give me your hand!" I reach over in bed as Zach grunts, just barely awake. "Come on give me your hand!"

I grab his palm and place it over my stomach. My skin is warmer than his and the touch is refreshing. After a few seconds, Zach sits up and looks at me, wide-eyed.

"Was that a kick?!"

"Yes! It just woke me up!"

Zach's eyes are still as big as saucers. He glances from my face to my stomach, moving his hand around gently. "Wow," he breathes.

The giggles burst out of me. "It's kicking! That's such a weird feeling."

"It's kicking so much! It has to be a boy!"

I roll my eyes. "It doesn't mean anything. And I know you, your heart would melt if you had a little girl."

"I don't care what it is," he says as he runs his hand up my body, cupping my breast and dipping his chin towards me.

"As long as it's healthy and you're healthy it doesn't matter what it is."

I smile as his lips touch mine. My happiness is complete. I've finally moved the last of my things into his apartment and we're having our first lazy Sunday morning in bed together in *our* apartment. I run my fingers over the scar on his chest and he shivers. He puts his hand over mine and we lay there, our hands over his heart, over his scar. I can feel his heart beating and I lean into him.

"Getting stabbed was the best thing that ever happened to me," he says. "Now I have this as a reminder of what I almost lost." Zach lifts his head up and strokes the side of my face. "I love you."

"I love you too. I wish you didn't get stabbed though," I grin. "There's lots of less painful reminders that I'm the best."

He smiles and then chuckles and my heart melts. I've never felt the kind of bursting feeling in my chest before. It's like I'm so full of love and happiness that I'm coming apart at the seams, like my body can't contain the sheer emotion that fills me up.

Zach runs his hand over my chest and down my arm. He spreads my hand and slides his fingers in between mine. His lips find mine and they fuse together. I'll never get sick of kissing him.

He grips my hand a little bit tighter and then pulls away, looking down at our interlocked fingers. He turns my hand around and watches as my grandmother's old ring glints in the morning light.

"You only ever wear that one ring."

"Yeah," I reply. "I've always worn it."

"Would you ever consider wearing another one?"

I frown and my heart starts beating a little bit faster. Is he saying what I think he's saying...?

"I mean... I guess?"

Zach grins. "What I mean is, if I gave you a ring would you wear it?"

"Are you asking me to marry you?"

"Would you say yes if I was?"

I laugh. "What is this, Sunday morning riddles? What are you saying, Zach? Spit it out."

"I'm saying marry me."

I can feel my eyes crinkling as the smile breaks my face open. If I felt like happiness was bursting through my chest before, I had no idea what I was in for. It feels like I'm about to float away, and the only thing holding me down is the weight of Zach's body over mine. My vision goes blurry as the tears of joy flood my eyes. All I can do is nod.

"Yes," I croak.

Zach's kiss is more ardent than ever before. Suddenly his lips are on mine, his hands are over my body. He strokes my stomach gently and then runs his fingers down over my mound to my aching centre. I wrap my arms around him and my legs fall open as his hand inches closer.

Every night we spend together is better than the last. Every touch is more intimate, every kiss is more passionate. I've never been this happy. That feeling reaches a new peak this morning. It feels like I'm vibrating with love, with emotion, with passion. I let myself be taken away by it, letting my hands sink into his flesh and my lips explore his body.

Our bodies start an intricate dance that only instinct can explain. His movements are my movements, his touch is electrifying and comforting and exciting and intoxicating all at once. My body spasms and contracts and his does the same.

209

My hands roam over his skin, hungrily touching every single inch of him. I can't get enough.

We grab and grope and touch and moan as we let ourselves be carried away. It's passion on another level. I throw my head back and listen to myself moan and say his name over and over. *Zach, Zach, Zach.*

I'm panting, he's groaning, I'm moaning, he's grunting. The sounds of our passion fill the room. I'm riding an indescribable high. His hands are everywhere, our bodies are fused together until finally we both fly over the edge together. I grab onto him and he grabs onto me and we don't let go until our heartbeat has gone back to normal. Even then, our legs stay intertwined and our arms are thrown over each other. My lips are near his and our breath mixes as we recover.

"I love you," I whisper.

"I've never loved anyone as much as I love you," he replies. He kisses the tip of my nose and I close my eyes. The baby kicks and Zach makes a noise.

"We love you too," he says, sliding his hand over my growing bump. His words send another shiver down my spine and I nuzzle my chin into his chest. Zach wraps his arms around me and I sigh contentedly.

I've moved into a new house and I've found a home, a husband, a family. I smile as I think of the doctor who told us we were pregnant. *Miracle baby*, he'd said. I'm starting to think he was right.

~

I hope you enjoyed Knocked Up by the CEO! I'd love it if you left a review to let me know what you think.

Grab your own exclusive bonus chapter to see how Harper and Zach are doing when their baby is born. All you have to do is go to http://eepurl.com/ddxnWL

∼

xox Lilian
www.lilianmonroe.com
Facebook: @MonroeRomance
Instagram: @lilian.monroe

Psst... Keep reading for a preview of Book 2

Knocked UP
BY THE SINGLE
DAD

A SECRET BABY
OFFICE ROMANCE

LILIAN MONROE

KNOCKED UP BY THE SINGLE DAD

A SECRET BABY OFFICE ROMANCE

Lilian Monroe

www.lilianmonroe.com
Facebook: @MonroeRomance
Instagram: @lilian.monroe

ROSIE

"COME ON, HARPER, STAY!" I plead, holding out my hands in front of me. Harper's jacket is almost on. She's got one arm through the sleeve and is reaching for the other one. "The babysitter can stay a little bit longer tonight. It's my birthday!"

"Yeah, Harper, stay!" Jess says, standing next to me and staring at Harper. Both of us are a good six inches taller than her but she doesn't seem phased. Harper sighs and purses her lips at me, but I can see the smile in her eyes. She puts her hand up, pointing her finger at me.

"Fine. One more drink. But only because you're my best friend and my daughter's godmother."

"Yay!" I exclaim, wrapping my arms around my best friend. Ever since she had a kid she always smells like babies. It's a comforting smell, sort of fresh and homely at the same time.

"So, Rosie," Jess says as she waves the bartender over. "How does it feel to be another year older."

"Feels like I was stabbed about six times," I respond.

They laugh, and then Harper looks at me with pain in her

eyes. I know she still blames herself for what happened to me, but she shouldn't.

A year ago, our ex-coworker kidnapped Harper and came after me. He held her hostage and came to my house and stabbed me in the chest and stomach six times. He was delusional and obsessed with Harper and thought I was trying to keep them apart. I was, in a way, but only as much as a someone trying to protect their best friend. He's locked up in a mental institution now, but it's still fresh in everyone's memory.

"At least you got some wicked scars," Jess says with a grin. I brush my hands over my rib, where the biggest jagged scar cuts across my body.

"They're fading now. You can hardly tell they're there!" I say, glancing at Harper. Her face relaxes and she smiles back.

It's a lie, of course. When I was getting dressed this morning I saw the same six angry red scars all over my chest and stomach. They mar my skin as a constant reminder of how close I came to death. I tug at the neckline of my shirt, pulling it up to make sure the scar above my heart is still concealed. It's become almost an unconscious movement now.

I smile at my best friend and she squeezes my arm in thanks. I know Harper is still struggling with the memories of it all even over a year later. I know she still struggles with being at home alone and with people coming up behind her. She hates surprises now. That's why I've never told her how much I've suffered over the past year, both physically and mentally. She has a new baby girl and she needs all the strength she can get. Besides, I can take care of myself.

Jess pulls me from my thoughts with a fresh drink, presented to me with a wink. I take it and smile, tucking a strand of my fiery red hair behind my ear before lifting the glass and tapping it gently against hers.

"You're far too serious for your birthday," Jess says. "This is the first time we've been able to celebrate in weeks! Months, even!"

"You're right," I respond with a smile. I shake my head and my red curls brush against my cheeks. I need to snap out of it. If not for my sake, for Harper's. It may be my birthday but she deserves a night away from the baby.

"We need to find you a man, is what we need to do," Jess announces. She spins around, surveying the room like an expert judge. I laugh.

"That's the last thing on my mind right now."

Jess shoots me a look and rolls her eyes. "Don't lie to me, Rosie."

The three of us laugh and Harper pokes me in the ribs with her elbow. I throw up my hands. I haven't been out in months and haven't had sex in who knows how long. Call it residual fear of people, or stress, or whatever. I've just been saying I'm busy with work, but the thought of letting a strange man into my apartment still makes me uneasy. Ever since the incident last year I haven't been the same.

"Fine! Fine! Yes, I need to get laid. But I'm not going to just jump into bed with anyone."

Jess turns those dark brown eyes towards me. She lifts an eyebrow and even though she looks sarcastic I know it's coming from a place of love.

"Rosie, not only do you need to get laid, you need to get royally Fucked with a capital 'F'."

Harper laughs and I can't help but join in. I shrug and nod my head, giving in. Jess dips her chin and turns back towards the bar.

"Now, who's gonna be the lucky man," she says almost as if she's speaking to herself. She taps her fingers against her chin and swings her eyes around the room.

"Come on, Jess, don't force it," I laugh.

"What about him?" She says, pointing across the room.

"Can you *be* more obvious?!" I protest, laughing. Her arm is extended and she's pointing straight at a group of men. "No. Definitely not," I say after glancing at the man. He looks over at us and our eyes meet for an instant. My cheeks immediately start burning. I look away and stare at Jess with my eyes wide. She grins.

"Okay, fair enough. I don't like his shirt anyways. What about him?" She asks again, pointing to another man.

Harper laughs. "Or him?" Now she's pointing to another man, both of them grinning from ear to ear.

I swat at their arms, laughing. "Guys, stop!"

"Well it's never going to happen with that attitude," Jess says with an exaggerated eye roll. She cracks a smile and shrugs, turning back to her drink. "You're just destined to be an old maid. I'm just trying to help."

"Nothing wrong with being independent," I respond, relieved that she seems to be distracted for now. I have no doubt she'll be back on the prowl for me in a few minutes. "I'm going to get us some drinks."

I breathe a sigh of relief when they let me go, still laughing and glancing around the room. I know for a fact there isn't a man in here I want to sleep with tonight, but I'll play along for now.

ROSIE

I SLIDE my way to the bar and try to catch the bartender's eye. I lean over and glance towards him, ready to tell him my order. I'm so focused on getting an opportunity to order that I don't see the man slide in beside me until he speaks.

"Buy you a drink?" He asks in a low growl. I almost jump out of my skin and whip my head around. It's the man with the awful shirt that Jess was pointing to. Great.

"No, I'm okay, thanks," I respond, turning back towards the bar.

"I saw you staring at me earlier."

My spine stiffens. I already said no, and here he is still talking to me. I swivel my head slowly and stare at the man. He's got dirty blonde hair and his shirt is a short-sleeved muddled brown and green plaid. He's got one too many buttons unbuttoned and I can see his unruly carpet of chest hair. It truly is one of the most revolting shirts I've ever seen.

"First of all, I wasn't staring. My friend was just commenting on your shirt. Second of all, I told you I'm not interested. Please leave me alone."

"My shirt?"

My jaw almost drops. Once again, this guy has ignored my blatant comment about not being interested. He's more concerned about his shirt than he is about the fact that I told him to leave me alone. I feel that familiar sense of panic rising in my throat.

Ever since the incident last year, strangers stress me out. Unfamiliar places stress me out. I glance around at my friends and see Jess and Harper deep in conversation. The man is still staring at me and the faint stench of his body odor starts making its way to my nostrils. My heartbeat is getting faster and faster as I turn back towards the bar.

"You were saying something about my shirt? What's wrong with it?"

My fear intensifies. He's not leaving me alone. I can almost feel the scars on my chest starting to burn, like a beacon warning me of danger.

This is why I don't go out! This is why I don't talk to strange men! They just can't take no for an answer and I'm left feeling vulnerable. The words catch in my throat and my body stiffens even more.

"You got those drinks yet?"

Jess's voice is the best thing I've heard in my life. It's like a lifejacket when I'm about to go under. She slides in between me and the man and turns her back to him. I glance over her shoulder and see the beginning of anger in his eyes, and I pray that he's not the type to get upset. I turn back to Jess.

"No, not yet. The bartender is pretty busy."

She nods and waves her hand. Within seconds, she has our drinks ordered and paid for. They arrive a minute later and we grab them, heading back towards Harper.

"What was that about?"

"He came up to me at the bar and asked why I was staring at him. I told him I was staring at his shirt and to leave me alone but he wouldn't take a hint," I respond. My heart is still pounding in my chest.

Jess puts an arm around my shoulder. "I'm sorry, Rosie. I was just trying to have a bit of fun. If you're not ready to be with a guy then you're not ready."

She hugs me and Harper puts her arm around me too. "We're here for you. However long it takes you to feel comfortable around people is fine. The fact that you're out in a bar is a big deal!"

I feel the tears gathering behind my eyelids. "Thanks Jess. I just don't think I'm ready to let a man into my house or into my life. I still start freaking out whenever someone talks to me."

She squeezes my shoulder and Harper clears her throat. Her eyes are filling with tears. I shake my head as a pang passes through my heart. The last thing I want to do is make Harper feel bad about it!

Jess shrugs. "I wouldn't worry about it, Rosie. His shirt truly is one of the ugliest things I've ever seen. It was even worse up close." She takes a sip of her drink and I start chuckling. Harper cracks a smile and Jess brings her drink down again. "And that chest hair! God! At least a trim! I'm not a fan of waxed chests, you know, I like a bit of chest hair on a man but even I have my limits!"

Jess shakes her head and now both Harper and I are laughing. My shoulders relax and I let the air out of my lungs. I know I was overreacting, but both Jess and Harper understand. Harper starts telling us about her daughter and the panic inside me dissipates completely. I know there won't be any more talk of men or getting laid tonight, and I'm glad.

LUCAS

"You sure you don't want to come out? It's your last night!" Max is looking at me expectantly, one eyebrow raised as he gauges my reaction. I try to smile but I think it might look like a grimace.

"Nah, I'll just take a cab to the hotel. Early flight tomorrow."

Max shakes his head and grabs his jacket. "Your loss, man. There's a lot of great women in New York City."

"Thanks, Max. I'm just tired tonight. Want to hit the ground running with this stuff when I get back to LA." I wave my hand across my desk at the neat stacks of paper that are ready to be packed into my bag. Max shrugs.

"Alright, well I'm going to head out. We'll be in touch later in the week for the launch."

"Have fun," I say as Max turns around and walks out. I sigh in relief. I couldn't think of anything worse than going out drinking tonight. His promise of 'great women' just makes me think of loud bars and loud women and people rubbing up against each other. I haven't met any 'great women' since my wife died, and I'm not sure they exist anymore. I just want to sleep.

I rub my eyes and run my fingers through my hair. My body is aching and I haven't even been to the gym all week. It was supposed to be a short business trip, over and back in two days, but it's stretched out to ten days, twelve to fourteen hours in the office every day.

We're launching my client's new music album in a week, and Max's advertising firm is the best in the country. I glance at the advertisement mockups and the schedules laid out in front of me and take a deep breath. The next few weeks will be completely manic, but they're crucial if we want this album to top the charts.

My phone buzzes and I smile as I see the name pop up.

"Hey kiddo," I say into the receiver.

"Dad! I got 98% of my math quiz today!"

"Wow!" I exclaim. "That's amazing!" I mean it too. I lean back in my chair and listen to my daughter as she tells me about her day. I smile and close my eyes.

"So you're going to be back tomorrow?"

"Yep, tomorrow afternoon. Can't wait to give you a big hug, Allie."

"Me too!" Her voice is full of energy. "I have a surprise for you!"

"A surprise!" I answer. "What is it?"

"I can't tell you, then it wouldn't be a surprise!"

I feel my shoulders relax and the smile spread from my face through my whole body. Ten days was far too long to be away from my little girl. She giggles and I feel that familiar warmth spreading in my chest whenever she makes me laugh.

"Okay, I gotta go, kiddo. I have to pack and get ready for my flight. I'll see you tomorrow."

"See you tomorrow, love you Dad!"

"I love you too, Allie."

We hang up and I sigh. Hearing her voice was exactly what I needed. Whenever I feel like I'm too focused on work she always reminds me of what's important, and tomorrow I get to see that little grin and kiss her cheeks. I stand up and start stacking my files. I slip them into my briefcase and then pack up my laptop.

I flick off the lights and look back at my temporary office. Hopefully I won't have to be back here for a long time. I'll get this album off the ground and take a few weeks off to spend with Allie.

When I step outside, the cool night air hits my face and I fill my lungs. I take a deep breath and smile. I'll be back home tomorrow.

I glance up and down the street and frown when I don't see a cab. I turn towards the nearest main road and let my feet take me there as my mind wanders back to LA, to our little house in the suburbs and to Allie's smiling face.

Ninety-eight percent! I think as I shake my head. She's smarter than her old man, that's for sure. I smile and turn my head just as a cab turns down the street. Perfect. I extend my hand and watch as he puts his indicator on and starts to pull over.

I glance down and see my shoe is untied. I wave at the cab until it starts to pull over and then bend over to tie my shoelace. I hum to myself as I tie my shoe, not paying attention to anything except the lightness in my heart. I'm going home, finally.

I hear a car door slam and I glance at the cab. He's still

there, so I stand up and start jogging over to it. Just a few more hours and I'll be with my little girl and out of the chaos of New York City.

ROSIE

"SEE you in the morning for brunch!" I call out as Jess and Harper head off in the opposite direction as me.

"Definitely!" says Jess. "Maybe the waiter will be hot and you'll have more luck getting laid tomorrow." She winks and I roll my eyes, laughing. She's relentless. I hope the waiters are all women and I won't have to deal with her jokes all day tomorrow. One night interacting with strangers was more than enough.

I turn back towards the street and wince as I take a step. My feet are aching from these ridiculous heels. My apartment is only a fifteen minute walk away but I might have to take a cab. It is my birthday, after all. I can be a little bit lazy tonight, of all nights.

I glance towards the street and sigh as I see a cab turning down towards me. I raise my hand and smile as the cab puts his indicator on and slows towards me. Perfect timing. I open the door and sigh as I sit down, easing the pressure on my feet. They're throbbing and I exhale as I slip my feet out of the heels. They definitely weren't this tight when I put them on a couple hours ago.

"Hi, can I go to—"

Before I can finish my sentence, the other back door opens and someone slips in. I immediately inhale his fresh, spicy scent and feel a warmth spreading in my core. The feeling surprises me and I can feel myself flushing as I realized what I'm feeling: the first stages of desire. That quickly turns to outrage as the man starts to speak to the driver.

"Hi, the Hilton by the airport please." His voice is deep and smooth. Before I can protest, the cab driver nods his head and starts moving.

"Excuse me!" I start. "What are you doing!" The warmth inside me turns to anger and indignation as I realize he's trying to steal my taxi.

The man turns his eyes to me and I'm almost knocked back. His face is chiseled with just a hint of stubble over his strong jaw. His eyes are a piercing blue and he stares at me with a complete calm.

"I'm going to my hotel. What are you doing in my cab?"

"*Your* cab?! I was very clearly in it first."

I see the cab driver glance at us in his rear-view mirror and frown.

"You two don't know each other?"

"No!" We answer in unison. I almost yell it, and the stranger says it as if it's a joke, as if the smile is playing just behind his lips. I shoot a glance at him sideways and feel something stir inside me when I see he's still staring at me. I push the feeling down and focus on my anger. The cab driver slows to a stop.

"So where am I goin'?"

"As soon as this man gets out I'll give you my address," I

respond, raising an eyebrow towards the door next to him. There's no way I'm saying where I live with him in here. He keeps his eyes on me and lifts his eyebrow in response.

"I'm not going anywhere. I was waiting for a cab on that street for ages. I have a flight to catch in the morning."

"Well you're not staying here. You can't just jump in a taxi that's already been taken!"

A smirk plays over his lips as his eyes travel down my body. I feel a shiver travel down my spine as his eyes take in every inch of me. Why do I like this feeling? I should be angry!

"How about this," he starts. "We drive to your place first, drop you off, and then I keep going towards the airport. We both get where we need to go, and I'll cover the fare."

I desperately want to say yes. His smell is intoxicating and I can hardly think straight with those eyes all over me. *Okay,* I think. *That sounds alright.*

"No."

He smirks again and I'm simultaneously annoyed and entranced.

"Why not?" He asks almost innocently.

"Yeah, why not?" The cab driver chimes in. We both ignore him, our eyes locked on each other. His question hangs in the air between us as the seconds tick by. I can't look away. His blue eyes drill into me and all I want is for him to look at me again. He licks his lips and the warmth in my core blossoms.

"Fine," I concede. The man's smirk spreads to a smile and he nods.

"Great. Where to?"

I sigh and give the cab driver my address. Sitting back in my seat, I stare straight ahead and try to ignore the pounding of my heart against my ribcage. My whole body is screaming at me to turn my head, to glance at him again. I can just see him in my peripheral vision, and it's taking every ounce of willpower to stop myself from looking at him.

He clears his throat and I close my eyes, trying to ignore the shiver that every sound and every move sends down my spine. I've definitely had one too many drinks. This feeling is not normal.

"Sore?" He asks softly.

I can't help it. I turn my head towards him and frown. "What?"

He nods to my feet. My shoes are off, my feet resting gently on top of them. I feel myself blush. I'm that typical drunk girl on her way home from the bar. I didn't even have that much to drink!

"Yeah."

I can't think of anything else to say. I can hardly think of anything except the throbbing between my legs growing to an ache whenever his eyes pass over me. Maybe Jess was right. I do need to get royally Fucked with a capital F if some stranger can have this effect on me.

Still, when I look at him I can't help but feel like he isn't just 'some stranger'. I haven't felt this comfortable around a man since before the incident with Harper's stalker. Usually I'd be nervous just being around a stranger, let alone saying my address in front of him. There's just something about him that makes me feel at ease. Maybe it's the way he's looking at me. There's a kindness in his eyes that makes me want to be near him.

"Here," he says in a low growl, holding out his hand. I don't understand so I just stare at him. He smiles more softly this time. "Give me your foot."

"What? I..." my voice trails off as his eyes bore into me. As if out of my control, I watch my leg shift and my foot lift up towards his waiting hand.

The instant my skin touches his hand it's like an electric current travels straight up my leg towards my center. The heat in my core intensifies and I feel my panties starting to soak through as his hand moves over my foot in slow circles.

I want him. My head is spinning. It's as if my body has a mind of its own and I'm just along for the ride.

I close my eyes and lean back. His touch is gentle at first, rubbing my heel and the arch of my foot. He uses both hands, completely covering my foot as he rubs it in smooth, long motions. My whole body relaxes as he moves his fingers up my arch towards my toes. I let out a soft groan and he chuckles.

The sound snaps me back to myself. I tense up and take my foot away, slipping it back into my shoes. I clear my throat and sit up, smoothing my dress down in front of me.

"That's okay, you can stop here," I say quickly. "I'll get out here."

"We're still five minutes away," the cabbie starts.

"That's okay, I'll get out."

"Whatever, lady," he says under his breath as he pulls over. I practically jump out of the cab and stumble towards the sidewalk, heart thumping and breath ragged. I vaguely hear the man yell out behind me but all I can do is rush down the street towards my apartment.

What. Just. Happened.

~

Thank you so much for reading. You can get the full version of Knocked Up by the Single Dad by finding me at https://www.amazon.com/author/lilianmonroe

Don't forget, you can get exclusive access to bonus chapters for ALL my books.
http://eepurl.com/ddxnWL

~

xox Lilian
www.lilianmonroe.com
Facebook: @MonroeRomance
Instagram: lilian.monroe